BANDITS
& REBELS

Publications of the North American Jules Verne Society

The Palik Series (edited by Brian Taves)

The Marriage of a Marquis
Contributors: Edward Baxter, Jean-Michel Margot, Walter James Miller,
Kieran M. O'Driscoll, Brian Taves

Shipwrecked Family: Marooned with Uncle Robinson
Translated by Sidney Kravitz; Introduction by Brian Taves

Mr. Chimp, and Other Plays
Translated by Frank Morlock; Introduction by Jean-Michel Margot

The Count of Chanteleine: A Tale of the French Revolution
Translated by Edward Baxter; Introduction by Brian Taves;
Notes by Garmt de Vries-Uiterweerd, Afterword by Volker Dehs

*Vice, Redemption, and the Distant Colony: Stories by Jules
Verne and Michel Verne*
Translated, with notes, by Kieran M. O'Driscoll

Around the World in 80 Days — The 1874 Play
Contributors: Philippe Burgaud; Jean-Louis Trudel, Jean-Michel
Margot, Brian Taves

Golden Danube
Translated, with notes, by Kieran M. O'Driscoll

(Other volumes in preparation)

**The North American Jules Verne Society also copublished
(with Prometheus)**
Journey Through the Impossible
Translated by Edward Baxter; Notes by Jean-Michel Margot

**Editorial Committee of the North American
Jules Verne Society:**

Henry G. Franke III   Dr. Terry Harpold
Jean-Michel Margot   Dr. Brian Taves

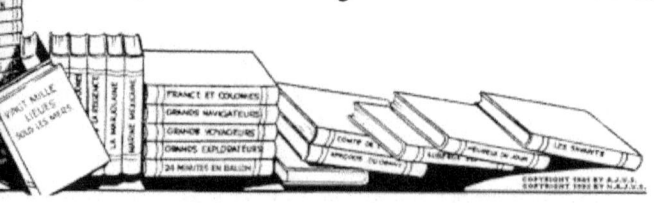

BANDITS & REBELS

by Jules Verne

Translated by Edward Baxter

Introduction by Daniel Compère

Edited by Brian Taves for
the North American Jules Verne Society

The Palik Series

BearManor Fiction
2013

Bandits & Rebels
by Jules Verne

Translated by Edward Baxter
Introduction by Daniel Compère

The Palik Series
Edited by Brian Taves
for the North American Jules Verne Society
najvs.org

For information, address:

BearManor Fiction
P. O. Box 71426
Albany, GA 31708

bearmanormedia.com

Typesetting and layout by John Teehan

Published in the USA by BearManor Media

ISBN—1-59393-395-9
978-1-59393-395-1

Table of Contents

This volume, containing Jules Verne's first submarine story, is dedicated to the first filmmaker to bring the author's undersea vision to the screen:

J. Ernest Williamson

Jules Verne in 1856.

INTRODUCTION

by Daniel Compère

Translated by Jean-Michel Margot
with Brian Taves

THE TURNING POINT in Jules Verne's literary career occurred in 1862 when, having met the publisher Pierre-Jules Hetzel, he began writing a series of novels known later as the "Voyages Extraordinaires" ("Extraordinary Journeys"). These comprise sixty-two novels and two anthologies published between 1863 and 1914. Today's reader is sometimes surprised when discovering previously written texts in which the author tried different avenues in writing. Many of these texts remained unpublished during Verne's lifetime, and while the manuscripts were known to Verne scholars, some were only published recently, including several short stories, plays and even novels.[1]

---

1. Of the novels, best known, because it was the only one to be science fiction, was *Paris au XXᵉ siècle* (*Paris in the 20ᵗʰ Century*). It had been written between 1860 and 1862, was rejected by Hetzel, and was published in France in 1994, with an English translation appearing in 1996. *Voyage à reculons en Angleterre et en Ecosse* (*Journey Backwards to England and Scotland*), the fictionalized account of the trip by Verne in July 1859, was published in France in 1989, with an edition appearing in the United Kingdom in 1993 as *Backwards to Britain*. It, too, had been turned down by Hetzel, as was *L'Oncle Robinson* (*Uncle Robinson*), not published in France until 1991; Verne had left it unfinished, rewriting it into *L'Île mystérieuse* (*The Mysterious Island*, 1874). This "first draft" did not appear in English until the translation for the Palik Series in 2011, retitled *Shipwrecked Family: Marooned with Uncle Robinson*, because Verne had subsequently used "Robinson" in a later, published title in the "Extraordinary Journeys." *Le Mariage de Monsieur Anselme des Tilleuls*, first published in Switzerland in 1993, was translated in English for the first time in the inaugural volume in the Palik series, *The Marriage of a Marquis*, in 2011. *Un Prêtre en 1839* (*A Priest in 1839*), a novel written between 1848 and 1849, briefly published in France in 1992, is to appear in its first translation in the Palik Series.

The short story "San Carlos" and the novelette *Le Siège de Rome* (*The Siege of Rome*) belong to the category of previously unpublished texts authored during the period when Jules Verne was improving his writing talent. In the 1850s, Verne was following two tracks: publishing short stories and composing for the stage. His encounter with Alexandre Dumas *père* in 1848 allowed him to present his first play, *Les Pailles rompues* (*The Broken Straws*), which opened June 12, 1850 at the Théâtre Historique in Paris. Comedies and operettas, with music by Aristide Hignard, followed during the 1850s, such as *Le Colin-Maillard* (*The Blind Man's Bluff*, 1853) and *Les Compagnons de la Marjolaine* (*The Companions of Marjoram*, 1855).[2] Verne's theatrical career benefitted from his position as secretary to the director of the Théâtre Lyrique, Jules Seveste, from 1851 to 1855: eight Vernian pieces were on stage there between 1850 and 1860, where the author used various styles, following the footsteps of Victor Hugo, sometimes Alfred de Musset, even Eugène Labiche; but the subjects are not original and the writing often banal.[3]

Less interesting are the pieces written around the year 1860, apart perhaps from the operetta performed at the Bouffes-Parisiens in 1858, *Monsieur de Chimpanzé* (*Mr. Chimpanzee*), which presents the ambiguity between man and ape, a theme appearing in a number of later stories, including "Gil Braltar" (1887) and *Le Village aérien* (*The Aerial Village*, 1901). Other productions of the same period, like *L'Auberge des Ardennes* (*The Inn of the Ardennes*, 1859), *Onze jours de siege* (*Eleven Days of Siege*, 1861), and *Un neveu d'Amérique ou les deux Frontignac* (*A Nephew of America or The Two Frontignac*, 1861) did not offer anything original.[4]

---

2. *Les Compagnons de la Marjolaine* was translated for the Palik series under the title, *The Knights of the Daffodil*, and appears in the 2011 volume collectively titled *Mr. Chimp & Other Plays*.

3. For an example of Verne writing in the vein of Hugo, see *Pierre-Jean*, rewritten and expanded by Jules's son Michel into *La Destinee de Jean Morénas* (*The Somber Fate of Jean Morénas*); both appear in the Palik series volume, *Vice, Redemption and the Distant Colony*.

4. *Mr. Chimpanzee* is the titular work in the Palik series volume, *Mr. Chimp & Other Plays*. *Eleven Days of Siege* also appears in this volume, which contains extensive background on Verne's theatrical career. Additional information on this subject appears in the North American Jules Verne Society's first book, the author's science fiction play, *Journey Through the Impossible*, published by Prometheus in 2002.

More interesting are the stories Verne wrote during the same time period. Most of them were published in the journal, *Musée des familles* (*Family Museum*), and suggested some of the future directions in Verne's writing. *Les premiers navires de la marine mexicaine* (*The First Ships of the Mexican Navy*, July 1851), "Un Voyage en ballon" ("A Balloon Journey," August 1851), *Martin Paz* (July-August 1852), *Maître Zacharius ou L'horloger qui a perdu son âme* (*Master Zacharius or The Watchmaker Who Lost His Soul*, April-May 1854), and *Un Hivernage dans les glaces* (*A Winter Amid the Ice*, April 1855). These last two stories, as well as "A Balloon Journey," retitled "Un drame dans les airs" ("A Drama in the Air"), were published, in modified form, some twenty years later in the anthology, *Le Docteur Ox* (*Doctor Ox*, 1874). Even as he let these early texts be republished, Verne was well aware of their flaws.

Verne then entered a period where he shifted gradually from the desire to imitate the oeuvre of Hugo, and away from the romantic style and the lightness of vaudeville. The stories published in this volume belong to a time when Verne was well aware he had not yet found his literary personality. Indeed, most texts written in this time were not published during his lifetime; in a way, they can be considered as exercises or sketches.

"San Carlos" is a short story probably written between 1860 and 1861. Compared to other stories written before, the reader discovers here a mature writing: Jules Verne portrays well-drawn characters and looks after the local color. San Carlos is a Spanish smuggler who, with his accomplices, brings cigars from Spain to France where they can be sold cheaper than those manufactured by the Régie des Tabacs (National Board of Tobacco). François Dubois, a French Customs Officer, tries to stop San Carlos by infiltrating his gang.

As the reader will discover, the hero defeats the perils posed by customs through the use of a ship where a valve can transform it into a submarine. Verne probably found the idea of this gear in the proposed rescue vessel invented by Jacques-François Conseil in 1857. On April 29, 1858, Conseil's boat made a thirty minute dive into the Seine between the Pont Neuf and the Pont Saint-Michel in Paris, with four members of the Académie Universelle des Arts et Manufactures (Universal Academy of Arts and Manufactures). In "San Carlos," the boat uses the same type of mechanism, an ellipsoidally-shaped sealed chamber communicating with the outside through a sliding panel. A few years later, Verne met Conseil at Le Tréport. Verne paid tribute by introducing him in *Vingt mille lieues sous les mers* (*Twenty Thousand Leagues Under the Seas*, 1870), although not as the inventor of the *Nautilus*, but as Aronnax's servant, still one of the novel's main characters.[5]

There is no indication when "San Carlos" occurs, but the action was likely intended to take place at the time of the writing of the story, around 1860. The story seems marked by a romanticist tone. I always thought that the hero's name referred to Don Carlos, a character in the famous Hugo play, *Hernani*, on stage in 1830, and considered the symbol of the romanticist revolution. The hero of *Hernani*, like the "San Carlos" of Verne, is an outlaw living in the mountains.

I propose to locate in "San Carlos" an ironic allusion to the famous poem "Le Lac" ("The Lake") by Lamartine, published in 1820 in the volume *Méditations poétiques* (*Poetic Meditations*). This poem is considered the true symbol of Romanticism.[6]

Un soir, t'en souvient-il? nous voguions en silence
On n'entendait au loin, sur l'onde et sous les cieux,
Que le bruit des rameurs qui frappaient en cadence
Tes flots harmonieux.

Tout à coup des accents inconnus à la terre
Du rivage charmé frappèrent les échos;
Le flot fut attentif, et la voix qui m'est chère
Laissa tomber ces mots:

"O temps, suspends ton vol! et vous, heures propices,
Suspendez votre cours!
Laissez-nous savourer les rapides délices
Des plus beaux de nos jours!"

("One evening we two roamed—remember?—in silence:
On waves and under heaven, far and wide,
No sound came save the cadence of the oarsmen
Stroking your tuneful tide.

---

5. Daniel Compère, "Conseil," *Bulletin de la Société Jules Verne*, No. 19 (1971).

6. Daniel Compère, "A la recherché des systèmes nouveaux, " *Bulletin de la Société Jules Verne*, No. 63 (1982).

Then sudden tones, unfathomed on this earth,
Resounded round the echoing, spellbound shore.
The tide turned heedful; and I heard these words
From the voice I adore:

"Suspend your trek O Time! Suspend your flights
O favoring hours, and stay!
Let us pause, savoring the quick delights
That fill the dearest day."[7])

There are some sentences and paragraphs in "San Carlos" that seem to be a distorted echo of Lamartine's poem: "Les huit hommes ramaient en silence. San Carlos dirigeait le bateau. Ils avançaient lentement sur cette onde immobile qui ne se prêtait d'aucune façon aux efforts du navigateur!... Soudain, un bruit inaccoutumé se fit entendre ! C'était celui de rames battant irrégulièrement l'eau !...—Ohé du bateau, cria une voix douée d'un accent français!" ("The eight men rowed in silence, with San Carlos guiding the boat. They moved slowly across the still water, which gave no help whatsoever to the efforts of the rowers... Suddenly they heard the unexpected sound of oars beating irregularly on the water...—'Ahoy! You in the boat!' cried a voice with a French accent.") As can be seen clearly here, Verne's text is built at the same time *with* Lamartine's poem whose words are in Verne's story, but also *against* the poem as a mockery of it: the meditation here is not on the passage of time, but the smuggling of tobacco.

When Verne wrote "San Carlos," Romanticism already seemed past to him—the movement that excited the past generation. Like his contemporaries, Gustave Flaubert, Charles-Pierre Baudelaire, and Isidore Lucien Ducasse (known as Comte de Lautréamont), Verne was in search of a literature more rooted in the modern world.

Another area demonstrates to me that the author is still in search of his métier. Introducing the character of San Carlos, the narrator describes him this way: "Un original sans copie parmi les types contrebandiers de l'Opéra-Comique." ("The smugglers in the cast of the Opéra-Comique included no one like him.") Costumes, disguises, and tricks are indeed elements that return us back to the theater Verne

7. Lamartine's poem was translated by A.Z. Foreman. http://poemsintranslation. blogspot.com/2010/04/lamartine-lake-from-french.html, accessed May 13, 2012.

knew and in which he long sought to make his career.

"San Carlos" demonstrates that Verne had mastered his writing style. He is able to describe the merging climate of the smugglers and the nature in which they live.

> Ces hommes, tranquilles comme les masses gigantesques qui pesaient sur leur tête, semblaient vivre de cette vie stable et accidentée des natures montagneuses; tantôt inébranlables, fixés au sol, sans mouvement appréciable, ils semblaient pétrifiés comme les rocs immobiles sur lesquels ils reposaient; tantôt vifs, fougueux, emportés, on les eût pris pour ces torrents éblouissants et rapides dont le Gave anime parfois les sinuosités folles et multiples de son cours. Au milieu de leur existence paisible ou remuante de contrebandiers, dans les engagements avec leurs redoutables ennemis, et pendant les répits de quelques heures que leur jetaient parfois l'ignorance ou la lassitude fiscale, ils étaient bien les véritables indigènes de ces montagnes perdues, les hommes de cette nature incompréhensible, faite de rochers, de torrents et de nuages.

> (These men, as quiet as the gigantic masses hovering over their heads, seemed to lead the stable but eventful life of mountaineers. Sometimes they would be steadfast and attached to the earth, apparently without moving. They seemed petrified, like the motionless rocks on which they lay. Sometimes they would be lively, spirited, and quick-tempered, like the swift, dazzling rapids to be found here and there in the course of the crazily winding Gave River. In the midst of their smugglers' life, whether calm or active, in encounters with their formidable enemies or during the few hours of respite that the ignorance or weariness of the customs officers sometimes conferred on them, they were the true native sons of those remote mountains, part of the mysterious nature of rocks, streams, and clouds.)

As the narrator himself points out, this story provides examples of "poésies grimpantes" ("creeping poems"), a particular writing of Verne where the object itself becomes language:

Quelques plantes hasardaient leurs jolies têtes entre les pierres moins serrées, et tenaient leurs beaux yeux fermés jusqu'au matin naissant. Les panaches flottants du saxifrage à longue feuille s'affaissaient avec mélancolie, et, dans leur sommeil, oubliaient la proximité rivale du panicaut cramoisi, et de la carline à feuilles d'acanthe. Des bruyères d'espèces variées confondaient çà et là leurs tiges silencieuses, les rhododendrons avaient éteint les rayons sans nombre qui, par les beaux soleils, vont puiser à la féconde corolle leurs couleurs les plus éclatantes, et les lys blancs, ayant mystérieusement rapproché les lobes de leur calice de satin, attendaient en silence le lever de la prochaine aurore pour adresser au ciel avec le chant des oiseaux et les actions de grâce de l'homme, leurs prières éblouissantes et leurs hymnes de parfums.

(A few plants timidly pushed their pretty heads up among the stones, wherever there was room, keeping their lovely eyes closed until morning. The fluttering plumes of the long-leafed saxifrage slumped mournfully to the ground, forgetting, as they slept, their nearby rivals, the purple thistle and the spiny-leafed acanthus. Various species of heather intermingled their silent stalks here and there. The rhododendrons had extinguished the countless rays of light which, in the bright sunshine, call forth brilliant colors from their fertile blossoms. The white lilies had mysteriously closed the lobes of their satin calyxes and were waiting in silence for daybreak before addressing to heaven their dazzling prayers and perfumed hymns, in harmony with bird songs and human prayers of thanksgiving.)

A question arises to any reader reading "San Carlos": Why was this well-constructed and well-written story unpublished for so long? Is it because it praises the character of an outlaw and therefore was not desired by the *Musée des familles* in the 1860s? In subsequent years, Verne never suggested publishing "San Carlos" to Hetzel—something that did occur for a number of stories published previously in the *Musée des familles*. Other short stories were also revised and reissued as an addition to some novels of the "Extraordinary Journeys." "San Carlos" was not even mentioned when Verne was considering, between

1891 to 1893, the release of a new collection under the title *Souvenirs d'enfance et de jeunesse* (*Recollections of Childhood and Youth*). Nor was it utilized by Verne's son, Michel, when he rearranged the proposed contents into the posthumously published anthology, *Hier et demain* (*Yesterday and Tomorrow*, 1910). For me, the only explanation remaining is that Verne considered "San Carlos" a draft, an outline of a possible work to come. As a result, "San Carlos" remained unpublished until 1993 when it appeared in France in the collection *San Carlos et autres récits inédits* (*San Carlos and other Unpublished Stories*). The same may be said for *The Siege of Rome*.

The Siege of Rome is a historical account showing Verne as a disciple of Dumas by putting fictional characters in a historical situation and in relation to people who actually existed, and in this instance, were in many cases still prominent, living individuals. The exact time when Verne wrote the story is unknown. An indication is given by the manuscript which bears the address 54 Faubourg Montmartre, where Verne was living from 1860 to 1861 before moving to 153 Boulevard Magenta, his address at the time of the birth of his son, Michel Verne, in August 1861.

Some scholars prefer the date of 1854, making a connection to *Rome et ses environs en 1853* (*Rome and its Surroundings in 1853*), published in *Le Musée des familles* (to which, as has been noted, Verne was a regular contributor). *Rome and its Surroundings in 1853*, signed by Mary-Lafon, recounts the drama of a young woman whose fiancé died during the siege of Rome. Verne probably read this text, but there is no way to tell if this story is the source of writing *The Siege of Rome*.

Another point to consider is the *Salon de 1857* (*Salon of 1857*), a series of articles of artistic criticism published by Jules Verne in *Revue des Beaux-Arts, Tribune des artistes* from June 15 to September 15, 1857.[8] Among the paintings reviewed by Verne is one by Horace Vernet, "Siège de Rome."[9] As noted by Volker Dehs in the preface to

---

8. These articles by Verne were recently republished with the title *Salon de 1857*. The complete text was prepared, presented and annotated by Volker Dehs in 2008 and is available at http://www.scribd.com/doc/6509469/Jules-Verne-Salon-1857-version-complete-et-revisee-de-Volker-Dehs.

9. Émile Jean-Horace Vernet (1789–1863) was a French painter of battles, portraits,

his edition of *Salon de 1857*, the full title is "Épisode du siège de Rome: prise du bastion no. 8 à la porte de San Pancrazio, le 30 juin 1849" ("An Episode of the siege of Rome, taking of the bastion no. 8 at the gate of San Pancrazio, June 30, 1849"). This 1852 painting shows the episode which ends chapter 4 of the Vernian novelette.

Verne's *The Siege of Rome* opens with a "historical prologue" in which Verne describes the context of the story. The plot is located in a time when what was then called "La Question romaine" ("The Roman Question") aroused much discussion.[10] The Republican movement, born in France in 1848, and headed by Mazzini in Italy, compelled Pope Pius IX to flee from his palace in Rome, the Quirinal, to Gaeta. Austria and France, two countries that had occupied Italy in the early 19th century, competed to help the Pope in his situation. France, led in the Second Republic by President, Louis-Napoleon Bonaparte, sent a military expedition to allow the Pope to return to the Vatican and regain his temporal power.

The reader follows the French expedition in which Henri Formont will meet Andreani Corsetti on the enemy side. He has taken Mary, Henri's bride, and holds her prisoner in an underground cell. The end is tragic.

Two elements are to be remembered from this story, which, from my point of view, lacks the qualities evident in "San Carlos." On one hand, there is a theme which will be found in future novels, the abducted woman, losing her reason, which matches with the characters of Ellen Hodges in *Une Ville flottante* (*A Floating City*, 1871) and

---

and Orientalist Arab subjects. In Sir Arthur Conan Doyle's Sherlock Holmes story, "The Adventure of the Greek Interpreter," Holmes claims to be related to Vernet, stating that "My ancestors were country squires... my grandmother... was the sister of Vernet, the French artist."

10. The Roman Question (in Italian: *La Questione romana*) was a political dispute between the Italian Government and the Papacy from 1861 to 1929. It began when Rome was declared the capital of Italy on March 27, 1861, and ended with the Lateran Pacts in 1929 between Mussolini's government and Pope Pius XI. After the capture of Rome on September 20, 1870, the popes considered themselves (in the words of Pope Pius IX) "prisoners in the Vatican." After the Lateran Pacts, the Popes regularly visited parts of Rome outside the Vatican. In particular, they took possession, after their election, of their cathedral, the Basilica of St. John Lateran, situated on the opposite side of the city. They also went to their summer residence at Castel Gandolfo, which has extraterritorial privileges, like an embassy, but is not part of the Vatican City State.

Laurence Munro in *La Maison à vapeur* (*The Steam House*, 1880). This theme makes *The Siege of Rome* part of the "roman noir" ("dark thriller") genre and close to one of the most famous, *The Mysteries of Udolpho* by Ann Radcliffe. Verne had read Radcliffe's novel, which tells the misfortunes of Emilia Saint-Aubert, trapped by an Italian brigand, Montoni.[11] When Emilia is locked in the castle of Udolpho, Montoni doesn't hesitate to threaten her physically.

The *Siege of Rome* expresses monarchist and Catholic ideas, quite similar to those found in another story that I think was written in the same year, 1860, *Le Comte de Chanteleine* (*The Count of Chanteleine*).[12] Nonetheless, *The Siege of Rome* also refers to the "shameful practices" of the Italian clergy who are pedophiles. The charge is clearly explained in a passage in chapter 1 where criticism of the Roman priests allows the author to praise those of France.

> Lorsque les ministres français pratiquent la vertu qu'ils prêchent, les nobles cardinaux ravissent et séduisent les je-unes enfants qui viennent implorer à leurs genoux le pardon de fautes vénielles; et alors que ces prélats opulents obli-gent quelque honnête cavalier à recouvrir de son honneur le déshonneur de leur victime, les prêtres de France mettent leur vie au service de toutes les infortunes, leurs bénédictions vis-à-vis de tous les efforts humains, leurs consolations en présence de toutes les douleurs, et sans repos, sans joie, sans plaisir, pendant leur pénible ministère, ils passent les nuits à prier pour les malheureux auxquels ils ont consacré leurs jours.

> (While French clergymen practice the virtue that they preach, the noble cardinals abduct and seduce young children who come on bended knee to beg forgiveness for their peccadillos. And while those wealthy prelates force some honest cavalier

---

11. Verne did not speak nor read English, but did read Radcliffe's novel in the French translation by Victorine de Chastenay and Jean-Baptiste Desprès (Paris: Maradan, 1819).

12. Originally published in the *Musée des familles* from October to December 1864, *The Count of Chanteleine* was first published in 2011 in English translation in the Palik series. For a more detailed account of the novel's composition, see the Afterword to that edition, by Volker Dehs.

to use his honor to conceal the dishonoring of their victim, the French priests devote their lives to every misfortune, bestow their blessings on all human endeavors, and offer their condolences in the presence of all suffering. During their arduous ministry, without rest, without joy, without pleasure, they spend their nights praying for the unfortunate ones to whom they have dedicated their days.)

It does not seem that real scandals happened in the 19th century, on a scale with those faced recently by the Catholic Church. However, it is true that rumors have spread at various times about pedophilia among priests. That said, I know few literary texts mentioning the subject, but a late novel by Émile Zola, *Vérité* (*Truth*, 1903), condemns the silence of the Church's hierarchy regarding such behavior among its ranks.

———•———

Martin Paz is included in this volume as an appendix because it is similar in genre to both "San Carlos" and *The Siege of Rome*, written around the same time, but unlike those two, *Martin Paz* was published contemporaneously with its composition—and not only in France, but in the United States as well. *Martin Paz* was the third published story by Jules Verne, appearing in the *Musée des familles* in two issues, from July to August 1852, with—as usual in this magazine—a subtitle: *L'Amérique du Sud. Mœurs péruviennes* (*South America. Peruvian customs*). Once Verne had become famous, *Martin Paz* was used to fill out the Hetzel volume including the short novel, *Le Chancellor – Journal du passager J.-R. Kazallon, Suivi de Martin Paz* (*The Chancellor – Diary of the Passenger J.R. Kazallon, Together with Martin Paz*) in 1875.

The text published here is the translation of the original version of the story; when Hetzel republished *Martin Paz*, it was slightly modified, and it was this later version, in translations by George Towle for the American edition and by Ellen Frewer for the British publication, that have hitherto been reprinted. Instead, this volume uses the original translation from *Musée des familles*, as it appeared in the April 1853 issue of *Graham's American Monthly Magazine of Literature, Art, and Fashion*, a publication from Philadelphia between 1844-1858. It appeared as "The Pearl of Lima, A Story of True Love, Translated From the French of M. Jules Verne" and followed "A Voyage in a Balloon" a year earlier; it was the second, and last, publication of a Verne story in English until 1867, when *De la Terre à la lune* (*From the Earth to the Moon*, 1865) was translated in the United States.[13]

The action of *Martin Paz* takes place in the 1830s, as indicated by the narrator's mention of "President Gambarra" in chapter 5. Agustin Gamarra was twice president of Peru, after Bolivar and Santa Cruz, from 1829 to 1833, and again from 1836 to 1841. A tragic love story unfolds: the Indian Martin Paz loves Sarah, daughter of the Jew, Samuel. Sarah, however, has been promised to a wealthy mestizo, Andre Certa. Sidelined by the Indians and his own father, the *Sambo*, Martin finds a protector in the noble Spaniard, Don Vegal. Martin will fight his own relatives, who regard him as a traitor, to protect Vegal and Sarah. Had Paz been born in North America, Verne notes in chapter 2, he would have been a great chief among those tribes who fought the Europeans displacing them from their lands. The denouement looks forward to the climax of Verne's 1889 novel, *Famille-sans-nom* (*Family Without a Name*).

Part of the background of *Martin Paz,* as reported by Pitre-Chevalier, the director of the *Musée des familles,* is the claim that it was written after pre-existing illustrations by Ignatius Mérino.

> Voyant le Pérou tout entier palpiter sur nos gravures, notre collaborateur, M. Vernes [sic], entouré d'ailleurs de tous les voyages d'outre-mer, renseigné minutieusement par tous les touristes liméniens, a écrit la nouvelle historique et pittoresque de Martin Paz, dans laquelle il a fait agir et parler tous les types créés par M. Mérino.

13. In the text here, minor typographical errors, inconsistent hyphenation, and spelling have been standardized, while variant and unique spellings remain as printed. The translation of *Martin Paz* was by Anne T. Wilbur, who had also translated Verne's "A Voyage in a Balloon" the previous year for a different Philadelphia journal, *Sartain's Union Magazine of Literature and Art*, in May 1852. (It appeared in London in *The Working Man's Friend and Family Instructor*, July 31, 1852.) ("Un Drame dans les airs" had first appeared in France the year before, and was retitled "Un drame dans les airs" for a slightly revised 1874 edition.) Anne Toppan Wilbur (1817-1864), whose married name was Anne T. Wood, also used the pseudonyms Mrs. Annie T. Wood, Mrs. John Procter, and Florence Leigh. Among her other translations from French into English are *The Solitary of Juan Fernandez; or, The Real Robinson Crusoe* (1851) and Théophile Gautier's *Le Roman de la Momie* (*The Romance of a Mummy*, 1863)—and she has the distinction of having translated both of the first known appearances of Jules Verne stories in English.

(Seeing the whole Peru palpitating in our images, our col-
laborator, Mr. Vernes [sic], surrounded by all the trips over-
seas, thoroughly informed by all the Lima tourists, wrote the
historical and picturesque short story of Martin Paz, in which
all characters created by Mr. Mérino act and speak.).

Pitre-Chevalier also presents the story as "un drame à la façon de
Cooper" ("a drama in the manner of Cooper"), which, at that time,
indicates a kind of adventure story today labeled the Western. France
enthusiastically discovered James Fenimore Cooper's novels, such as
The Last of the Mohicans, in the 1820s. It took several years more for
the French public to produce stories presenting French characters in
America, including *Les Chercheurs d'or* (*The Gold Diggers*, 1848) or
Costal l'Indien (*Costal the Indian*, 1852) by Gabriel Ferry, *Antoine Pin-
chon* (1832) by Jules Janin, and even *The First Ships of the Mexican
Navy* (1851), the first novelette by Verne.

In *Martin Paz*, money and religion are two subjects that place the
characters in opposition or unite them. The poor Indians are preparing a revolt against the rich, who are close to the Spanish mestizos like
André Certa. In between is the Jew, Samuel, whose portrait is in accordance with a certain anti-Semitic and anti-capitalist point of view that
was popular in the early 19th century. Chapter 3 has a description: "Ce
vieillard trafiquait de tout et partout; il descendait du Judas qui livra son
maître pour trente deniers!… Peu à peu, Samuel afficha un luxe inusité
aux avares; sa maison fut somptueusement entretenue et meublée; ses
nombreux domestiques, ses brillants équipages prouvèrent des revenus
immenses." ("This old man trafficked everywhere and in everything;
he might have been a descendant of the Judas who sold his Master for
thirty pieces of silver.… By degrees, Samuel assumed a luxury uncommon in misers; his house was sumptuously furnished; his numerous
domestics, his splendid equipages betokened immense revenues.")

The chapter which contains this portrait is entitled "Le Juif partout Juif" ("The Jew everywhere a Jew") and is shocking today. However, it is necessary to remember that the French mindset for many
centuries connected the Jews with usury. The Catholic Church forbade
Christians to lend money with interest, and only the Jews engaged in
the practice. As recalled by the historian Michel Winock, in the 19th
century, this state of mind was combined, in the Catholic as well as in

the socialist population, with anti-capitalist ideas and feelings.[14] The utopian socialist Charles Fourier suggests in his *Le Nouveau Monde industriel et sociétaire* (*The New Industrial and Social World*,1829) the exclusion of Jews from the phalanstery because of this wrong doing: "est de s'adonner exclusivement au trafic, à l'usure, et aux dépravations mercantiles" ("to engage exclusively in traffic, usury, and mercantile depravity").[15] Karl Marx in *Zur Judenfrage* (*The Jewish Question*, 1844) asserts that "Das Geld ist der eifrige Gott Israels, vor welchem kein andrer Gott bestehen darf" ("Money is the jealous god of Israel, before whom no other God must exist").[16]

This figure of the Jewish usurer may be found in many literary texts, for example in the novel *Gobseck* (1830) by Honoré de Balzac, or *Oliver Twist* (1837-39) by Charles Dickens, in the character of Fagin. The Samuel of *Martin Paz* belongs to the same tradition, which would have been expected by the Catholic readers of the *Musée des familles*. In a similar way, its readers would have been relieved by the final scene of the story, where it is revealed that Sarah has converted to Catholicism. The portrait of Samuel will be slightly reduced in the second version of *Martin Paz* in 1875, and the phrase "The Jew everywhere a Jew" eliminated.

That said, I share Francis Lacassin's opinion on this point. The anti-Semitism of Verne is "inexcusable" (the same word in both English and French), even if "alors partagé par la France quasi unanime" ("then almost unanimously shared in France"). However, Verne's prejudice is "balancé par la sympathie de l'auteur pour ces amours inter-raciales et impossibles" ("balanced by the sympathy of the author for inter-racial and impossible love").[17] *Martin Paz* is the first manifestation of Verne's interests for oppressed peoples, with its tale of conflicts among all the

---

14. Winock Michel, *La France et les Juifs de 1789 à nos jours* (Paris: Editions du Seuil, 2004).

15. Charles Fourier, *Le Nouveau Monde industriel et sociétaire* (Paris: Bossange *père*, 1829), 499; Charles Fourier, *Le Nouveau Monde industriel et sociétaire* (Paris: Anthropos, 1966), 421.

16. Karl Marx, *Zur Judenfrage* in *Deutsch-Französische Jahrbücher*, N° 1 (February 1844), 375; translated in Lawrence H. Simon, ed., *Karl Marx—Selected Writings* (Indianapolis: Hackett, 1994), 24.

17. Francis Lacassin, "Introduction: Jules Verne et les 'majorités opprimées' (1852-1905)," in Jules Verne, *L'Invasion de la mer, suivi de Martin Paz*, collection "10/18" (Paris: U.G.E., 1978), 11.

society's ethnic groups, and a range of types among each is offered within the narrative.

———•———

In *The Siege of Rome*, the character of the bandit Andreani Corsetti is revealed in chapter 1. He is a "figure basse et méchante" ("man with a mean and evil face"). He is "un de ces italiens faux, hypocrites, hardis au mal, inaccessibles au bien, vivant de cette nature ultramontaine si basse, si rampante, si envieuse, si lâche, si perfide" ("one of those false, hypocritical Italians, inured to evil, impervious to good, living on that ultramontane nature that is so low, so groveling, so envious, so cowardly, so treacherous"). After serving as secular secretary to the pope, he turned traitor and joined the camp of the rebels. "Qu'il était loin de ses salutations et de ses génuflexions contrites d'autrefois ! Il avait retourné son habit, et cela ne le changeait guère, car son habit était sale des deux côtés." ("How far he had come from his greetings and contrite genuflections of the past! He had become a turncoat, and that did not change him at all, because his coat was dirty both inside and out.") In chapter 5, the reader will also discover that Andreani Corsetti is a cruel executioner who has locked Marie in an underground prison. "C'était là que chaque soir, comme un tigre épiant sa proie, pour voir s'il ne lui reste pas quelque vie au fond du cœur, Andreani venait épier l'intelligence de la malheureuse ensevelie dans ce corps souffreteux et amaigri." ("Every evening, like a tiger eyeing its prey to see whether there is any life left in its heart, Andreani went there to spy on the intelligence of the unfortunate woman locked up in that sickly and wasted body").

André Certa, Martin Paz's enemy, is not a robber, even if he is the rival of the hero and introduced in a very unflattering way in chapter 1. André Certa is a young mestizo of swarthy complexion, with a thin beard that gives a singular appearance to his countenance. He is of mixed race, between two nationalities, sharing the mestizo sentiment. "Espagnols par le mépris qu'ils jetaient aux Indiens, Indiens par la haine qu'ils avaient vouée aux Espagnols, se consumaient entre ces deux sentiments vivaces et fougueux" ("Spanish in their contempt for the Indians, and Indian in their hatred which they had vowed against the Spaniards, burned with both these vivid and impassioned sentiments"). Like a traitor in a melodrama, he falls at the end, killed by Martin Paz.

In contrast, San Carlos is a sympathetic villain. If he lacks the fascination of the bandits of *Les Mohicans de Paris* (*The Mohicans of Paris*, 1855) by Alexandre Dumas and of the characters of Sir Williams and Rocambole in *Les Drames de Paris* (*The Dramas of Paris*, 1857-1859) by Pierre Alexis Ponson du Terrail, he adumbrates the ambiguous outlaws Verne will portray.[18] I refer in particular to Ayrton, proud and courageous in *Les Enfants du capitaine Grant* (*The Children of Captain Grant*, 1867), but also a pirate who attempts to seize Lord Glenarvan's ship. Verne places Ayrton in another novel in which he can rehabilitate himself, *L'Île mystérieuse* (*The Mysterious Island*, 1875). I also think that Nemo is an ambiguous pirate figure, but one whose behavior is motivated by the death of his family and the conquest of his homeland, leading to a desire for revenge (*Twenty Thousand Leagues Under the Seas*, *The Mysterious Island*). The character of San Carlos lacks the stature of these two, but anticipates them.

I believe that *The Siege of Rome* and "San Carlos" are, as I suggested, sketches of Verne's works yet to come. For me, it is significant that at no time, did the author of "Extraordinary Journeys" plan to publish them—unlike *Martin Paz*.

When he wrote these in the 1850s, Verne already had many writing qualities. He knew how to obtain the background information and documentation he needed from reliable sources. However, it seems to me that he still lacked the ability to put some distance from his own writing activity, which later would make his work unique and inimitable. Verne found this way of writing only in 1862, with *Cinq semaines en ballon* (*Five Weeks in a Balloon*).

From this viewpoint, it is worth recalling how Hetzel introduced a novelette such as *Martin Paz* in explaining the background of the story. In the note preceding the new version of the story, following *The Chancellor* in 1875, the publisher wrote:

---

18. Pierre Alexis, Viscount of Ponson du Terrail (1829-1871), was a prolific French novelist, producing in the space of twenty years some seventy-three volumes, and is best remembered today for his creation of the fictional character of Rocambole.

L'auteur n'avait pas encore trouvé le genre qu'il a créé et qui a rendu son nom célèbre. Mais il est curieux de le suivre dans ces essais. Ils contiennent déjà quelques-uns des germes qui font de l'œuvre générale de Jules Verne une œuvre à part dans notre littérature, et à ce titre ils méritaient d'être conservés.

(The author had not yet found the genre he created later and which made his name famous. But it is interesting to follow him in his attempts to get there. They already contain some of the germs that make the general work of Jules Verne a work unique in our literature, and as such they deserve to be preserved.).[19]

"San Carlos," *The Siege of Rome*, and *Martin Paz* are stories which cannot be ignored. All three contain themes and topics Verne would use and amplify later. They allow us to imagine the novelist whose career is about to begin. And even with their imperfections, they still deserve our attention because of their intrinsic qualities, as well as for the *absence* of what Verne will discover *after* having written them, once he began the "Extraordinary Journeys."

✛

19. A rather free translation was included as a footnote in the November 1875 edition published in England by Sampson Low. "*Martin Paz* is one of M. Verne's earliest works.... Previous to the publication of *Cinq Semaines en Ballon* the author had... not then adopted the style which has since rendered his name famous; but it is interesting to note how these first essays already indicated the germs of that genius which has made his works a specialty in our literature. For this reason they merit being preserved."

SAN CARLOS

Translated by Edward Baxter

"IS JACOPO BACK YET?"

"Not yet. It's two hours now since he left for Cauterets. He must have taken some long detours to explore the region."

"Does anyone know if old Cornedoux is still running his ferry across Lake Gaube?"

"Nobody knows, captain," replied Fernand. "It's nearly three months since we went through the Broto valley.[1] Those damned customs guys know all our hideouts, and we've had to stop using the usual paths. But after all, is there any crevasse in the Pyrenees, or any port, that you aren't thoroughly familiar with?"

"That's right," answered Captain San Carlos. "But even if I didn't know this country at all, hesitation would have been out of the question. Over by the eastern Pyrenees we were pursued day and night. We had to run countless risks and use almost impossible tricks in order to earn even a bare daily subsistence. When your life is at stake you have to win it, but out there we were on the point of losing it. And that Jacopo still isn't here! Hey, you there!" he called, turning to a group of seven or eight men leaning against a huge block of granite.

At the sound of their leader's voice, the smugglers turned to him.

"What is it, captain?" one of them asked.

"You know that we've got ten thousand *prensados* to smuggle across the border.[2] That means ready cash. You'll be glad to let the tax-man give us that charitable donation."

---

1. The Broto Valley is a town in the Spanish Pyrenees, south of Vignemale peak.

2. Prensados are packages of pressed tobacco.

"Bravo!" cried the smugglers.

"We left Jaca without too much trouble, and by avoiding the Saragosse road, and leaving it on our right, we reached Salient this morning.[3] That's where we took delivery of the merchandise, divided among these various bags. We got to the Broto Valley. Even though the area was swarming with green-jackets, we managed to cross the French border. Here we are now a day's journey from Catarave, where we'll deliver our goods and collect our pay in good coin of the realm."[4]

"Let's get going, then," said the most alert members of the band.

"Just a minute!" continued San Carlos. "The hardest part is still ahead of us. We're camped two leagues from Lake Arastille and Lake Gaube, with the road to Cauterets on our left.[5] If we can get to those lakes, we'll easily shake off any customs men that might be on our trail. There's a certain boat there that I know about, belonging to a man named Cornedoux. He could play lots of tricks on them, and in a few hours our tracks would be lost in the Geret woods."[6]

"So you've got a map of the area, have you, captain?" asked one of the smugglers.

"Yes, don't worry about a thing. Leave it all up to me, and I'll get you out of this dangerous spot."

"At your service, captain. What are your orders for the next quarter hour?"

"Make sure your weapons are in good condition and put fresh powder in your pans. It will soon be night, and the dampness would give our damned pursuers an advantage. It's bad luck that Jacopo isn't back yet. Remember, these *prensados* are like foreign noblemen; they have to get into France without paying a fee. But take care that their arrival isn't greeted with a few gunshots. Check the flints on your guns and have them ready to answer the first challenge.... What's that I hear in the distance?"

San Carlos interrupted his list of orders and put his ear to the ground.

---

3.   Salient de Gallego, the last Spanish settlement before the Pourtalet Pass.

4.   Catarave is a place-name based on Catarrabes, a village located north of Cauterets.

5.   Lake Arastille is a place-name based on Lake Arratille, four kilometres southwest of Lake Gaube.

6.   The Geret woods is a wooded valley between Cauterets and the Pont d'Espagne.

The Cirque de Gavarnie.

"It's Jacopo's footstep," he said as he stood up. "I recognize it. But he has to climb up the opposite slope of the mountain peak. He'll be here in half an hour. Take a rest now. Have courage and be careful. Sleep, my friends, sleep soundly and keep one eye open. I'll wake you when the time comes. *Buenas noches.*"

"*Si Dios quiere.*"[7]

Like overgrown, obedient children, the smugglers wrapped themselves in their coats, keeping their weapons within reach. Exhausted after carrying their merchandise over several leagues, they were soon asleep.

Captain San Carlos was still deep in thought, sitting near a large rock.

Night was falling over the Broto Valley and its dark arrival was accompanied by silence. The lower part of the glaciers was filled with a damp shadow, while on the horizon the snow-covered peaks of Estour still gleamed in the last light of day.[8] It was nine o'clock. The sky had extinguished all its stars and hidden its nocturnal wonders be-

---

7. "Good night."
   "If it is God's will."

8. Estour, for Estom Peak, in the Vignemale massif.

hind a thick curtain of profound darkness. The weather was turning dull, with the heaviness that sometimes hangs over the last months of autumn, but the massive clouds, which seemed to be held in place by the jagged mountain peaks, concealed no storm in their motionless blackness. With the approach of winter the temperature was already falling, but the ground, still warmed by the last rays of the September sun, amply compensated for the first chills brought on by the accumulated mists. There was hardly a breath of wind, as if the atmosphere were following the example of the smugglers, sleeping so silently that their slumber would not have betrayed them three paces away. These men, as quiet as the gigantic masses hovering over their heads, seemed to lead the stable but eventful life of mountaineers. Sometimes they would be steadfast and attached to the earth, apparently without moving. They seemed petrified, like the motionless rocks on which they lay. Sometimes they would be lively, spirited, and quick-tempered, like the swift, dazzling rapids to be found here and there in the course of the crazily winding Gave River. In the midst of their smugglers' life, whether calm or active, in encounters with their formidable enemies or during the few hours of respite that the ignorance or weariness of the customs officers sometimes conferred on them, they were the true native sons of those remote mountains, part of the mysterious nature of rocks, streams, and clouds.

Captain San Carlos's little band was huddled together in a sort of aerie formed by a crevasse hidden among inaccessible mountains. A path clinging to the south face of the mountain, and known only to the chief, provided a vertiginous access to the spot. An enormous pine leaned over this unlikely hiding place, making it almost impossible to discover. Apart from the captain, only Lady Luck, that two-faced traitor who passes constantly from one enemy camp to the other, knew about the obscure, stone-covered path.

From this hideaway, the gigantic barrier between France and Spain, the mountain range that slashes across the horizon for a distance of ninety leagues, could be seen in the distance at sunup. To the southwest, the Brêche de Roland, at whose base the smugglers had spent the previous evening, rose 1460 meters into the clouds.[9] The bizarre ridge along its flanks would have caught the viewer's attention, but the eye would have sought in vain for the summit of Mont Perdu,

---

9. The Brèche de Roland overlooks the Gavanie Cirque.

the highest peak in the Pyrenees, whose dizzying heights are eternally wrapped in their white mantle of snow.

To the north, the innumerable branches of the Gave River, the charming lakes set in those enchanting valleys, the thickets growing here and there on the hillsides, would have made a picturesque contrast to the rugged wonders of the south. It was a return to a gentler and more peaceful nature. Simply by climbing back down, one would find cultivated fields and cultured minds, but to reach Captain San Carlos's aerie, there were enormous rocky ledges to be scaled. Jacopo could not get there any sooner.

From *Le Phare du bout du monde* (*The Lighthouse at the End of the World*, 1905).

While he waited, San Carlos maintained his thoughtful pose. He was a small, thin, nervous man, quite undistinguished in appearance. The smugglers in the cast of the Opéra-Comique included no one like him. He was astute and inflexible by nature, a thief by necessity, and a prolific inventor of mathematically woven plots. His campaign strategies were nothing more nor less than daring theorems, which he solved using the principles of practical geometry. Those difficult problems of the trade were presented in advance to his comrades for their thoughtful consideration. He never depended on circumstances to bring out that instinctive genius that gives birth in desperate cases to the most wonderful schemes. But there were no desperate cases for Captain San Carlos. Every difficult situation had already been foreseen and had a ready-made solution, so that when danger threatened, the chief's shrewdness never failed him.

His comrades knew very well what kind of a man their commander was, and they had implicit faith in him. San Carlos controlled his group of semi-bandits, not by physical strength, but by strength of will. He was also physically dexterous, alert as a chamois and agile as an izard, and he knew how to handle his long-barreled firearm, whose range came as an unpleasant surprise to any green-jacket who had a painful experience with it. Like the others, he wore a colored jacket and trousers, with a carefully sharpened hunting knife stuck in his belt. A broad-brimmed hat extended over the colored silk net bag that hung on his back. A kerchief tied around his neck and light sandals on his feet completed his ensemble. His rifle lay nearby and his coat had been carelessly thrown on the ground among the leather bags containing the illegal merchandise. While his comrades slept, he waited patiently.

A low cry was heard, produced by quivering lips. San Carlos replied and soon Jacopo was standing beside him.

"Well?"

"Bad news!"

"All the better."

"Why?"

"Because if the news is bad, I'll be able to take decisive action. Good news would be deceiving and leave me up in the air."

"The customs boys are looking for us. They know about our expedition."

"We'll give them the slip."

"God willing."

"How far did you go?"

"As far as the lakes."

"And what about the ferryman?"

"I couldn't see him. The green-jackets were prowling all around."

"We'll cross the Cauterets road and come back to Lake Gaube farther up. That way we'll avoid the branches of the Gave River that run through the Geret woods."

"How will we get across the lake?"

"Don't worry about that, Jacopo. We'll meet up with the customs boys before we get there."

"Damn!" said Jacopo. "That's too bad!"

"Why?"

"Because Sergeant François Dubois, who kept us on the run in the Cerdagne, has been following our trail. He's sworn by all the gods that he'll take you dead or alive, and he's in command of the detachment at the Arastille lakes."

"I'll see about that."

"You know, captain, there's practically a price on your head. That gun of yours spoke a little too loud at our last meeting, so loud, in fact, that it silenced more than one of the enemies who were after us.."

"Don't worry about me. Wake the others and let's get going."

"I didn't come here alone, captain," said Jacopo, putting his hand on San Carlos's arm. "I've got a man with me who'd like to make a deal for a bag or two of cigars."

"Fine! Bring him along. And tell everyone to get ready."

Jacopo went away and San Carlos, left to himself, thought for a moment, rubbing his hands.

"We'll be worthy of the honor that Monsieur François Dubois has seen fit to bestow on us," he said. "I wouldn't mind making his acquaintance."

Jacopo came back, followed by a mountain peasant, and then went off to wake his comrades.

"Are you the leader?" asked the peasant.

"What if I am?"

"Is there any way I can make a deal with you?"

"Well, what do you want?"

The Brêche de Roland.

"Since you sell your goods to the merchants in the towns, you can easily spare a few for me, if I offer you a good price."

"That depends. What goods do you want?"

"Why… the stuff you've got here."

"What stuff?"

"Cigars."

"Who told you that?"

"Nobody. A smuggler always has cigars."

"How many do you need?"

"A thousand."

"Where are you going to sell them?"

"Over by Tarbes. That way, I'll save the commission that the merchants in Catarave make by selling the goods back to us."

"Well, we can work something out, but…"

"But what?"

"How are you going to get to the next town?"

"That's not hard."

"And how will you get past the customs?"

"I'll follow you, of course!"

"Ah!"

"I only came on ahead to make sure of your promise."

"But do you know who I am?"

"What a question! You're San Carlos."

"San Carlos? Whoever told you that?"

"The customs officers, of course."

"The customs officers? Where are they now?"

"Near the Arastille lakes."

"Did you see them?"

"As clearly as I see you now, Captain San Carlos."

"All right. Wait here."

"Jacopo!" he shouted

When Jacopo came up to him, the captain took him a few paces away from the peasant and said in a low voice, "Where are the customs guys?"

"At the Arastille lakes."

"Are you sure of that?"

"Absolutely."

"And you didn't tell that to this man here?"

"No, I didn't talk to him at all."

"Did he seem anxious to talk to you?"

"He didn't open his mouth."

"Where did you meet him?"

"On the Cauterets road."

"And what did he say to you?"

"He said 'I need some cigars.' And I said, 'Come with me.'"

"Let's go."

San Carlos went back to the peasant.

"You'll follow us," he said. "We'll settle matters on the way."

"As you wish."

The captain turned to his men, who were now on their feet. They had slung their coats and rifles over their shoulders and tied the bags of merchandise to their backs with artistically crossed ropes.

It was now pitch dark. The path was narrow and rocky and seemed to be attached haphazardly to the mountain side, sometimes running along the edge of a bottomless precipice. Their feet stumbled on the rolling pebbles that flashed sparks when they were struck. They had to walk in single file along that unsteady route. San Carlos led the way, followed by the peasant, who was followed in turn by two other smugglers. It required a thorough familiarity with the lofty twists and turns to prevent them from falling to their death.

The captain walked confidently among the huge projecting rocks and made his way without hesitation along the desolate secret paths. After a quarter of an hour he turned to the left and came to the foot of an almost vertical cliff, which had to be climbed.

Fastening iron crampons to their feet, the smugglers began the ascent. By means of those supporting spikes, they reached the top without too much difficulty. The peasant followed their example, using the same equipment.

"You're used to trips like this," San Carlos said to him.

"Yes, I am. This isn't the first time I've been along here."

"Really?"

"Really. I used to do business with Captain Urbano before he was stopped by the French smugglers. He sold me cigars at a good price and I paid him well. Did you know Urbano?"

"Yes. He was a decent chap, and if there hadn't been treachery involved, he'd still be shooting it out with those damned customs agents."

"He had a tough sergeant to deal with."

"Who was that?"

"François Dubois. He has quite a reputation, of course. Now he's in charge of the gates at the Cerdagne."

"No he isn't. He's over by the Arastille lakes."

The peasant was astonished. "That's impossible," he said.

"And he's sworn to take Captain San Carlos, dead or alive."

"Watch your step then captain. With all due respect, I wouldn't give much for your merchandise.."

"Why not?"

"Because there's a good chance it will never make it to Catarave – any more than you will."

"You think so?"

"Well, why don't we just say that nothing has happened and that I haven't asked you for anything? I'll get along without your cigars and you'll get along without my company."

"Coward! This Dubois must be really dangerous."

"Ah! You don't know him."

"No. He found out that the customs agents couldn't get the better of me and my men, and he followed me into the Cerdagne. But he couldn't catch up with me. Anyway, he seems to be a decent chap, so I respect him, and I'm delighted to match wits with him again. His tricks against mine. My skill against his. We have the advantage, because it's easier to set an ambush than to find it. Sergeant Dubois will never take Captain San Carlos."

"Why?"

"Because he boasts too much about capturing him."

The band was approaching the Cauterets road from the left and had now almost reached it. The smugglers stopped and San Carlos went to reconnoiter. The peasant wanted to go with him.

"You stay here!" said the captain.

"Please! Let me leave."

"No way!"

"Why not, captain?"

"Because you're a bit more of a coward than most."

The peasant made no reply and stayed with the smugglers. San Carlos walked along the road. Everything seemed quiet. On both sides there were huge piles of stones that would be hard to get over. To anyone else it would have seemed simple to follow the beaten track, since the customs agents were lying in wait in the rougher paths. But San Carlos had his plan, and motioned to his comrades to follow him.

"What road is this?" he asked the peasent.

"The road to Cauterets."

"Good," said San Carlos.

They crossed it and set out over the almost supernatural-looking heaps of stones and boulders. The battlefield on which Jupiter defeated the coalition of giants must have been strewn with missiles that were thrown back at them. Near the enormous boulders, which only the hand of Enceladus could have upended, motionless cataracts of stones jutted out from the sides of the road.[10] These rounded pebbles must have fought noisy battles with each other during storms in the Pyrenees. The silence that hung over so many carefully balanced rocks contrasted sharply with the haughty heaps whose every crack held an echo that exploded like thunder. After half an hour San Carlos's men stopped. They had reached one of those secret hiding places where the smugglers hastily concealed their illicit merchandise when they were being pursued too closely. San Carlos made the peasant step back a few paces and checked to make sure the crevasse was empty. Then he

---

10. Enceladus is one of the giants to which Gaia gave birth to take revenge for the defeat of the Titans. He in turn was defeated by Zeus and buried beneath Mt. Etna, whose eruptions are caused by his breath.

From *The Lighthouse at the End of the World.*

rejoined his comrades and told them to put all the bags they been carrying together in one place.

"How many cigars do you want?" he asked the peasant.

"A thousand, if possible."

"And how much will you pay for them?"

"Well, captain, your merchants sell them in France for four *sous*, and the state-owned company sells them for five. I want to double my money."

"That will be thirty *écus*" said San Carlos.

"Twenty-five. That's my best offer."

"Thirty *écus*, my friend. That's the lowest price you can pay for *prensados* smuggled past Sergeant Dubois."

"God help me," said the peasant. "They haven't got to their destination yet. Twenty-five *écus*, cash. I'll resell them for fifty and make a clear profit of seventy-five francs."

"It's a deal. Take one of these bags. They hold a thousand."

The peasant made as if to open the bag.

"You don't trust us," said the captain.

"Of course I do, but business is business."

"As you wish. But where's the money?"

"Here are fifteen good French coins."

"Haven't you got any Spanish money?"

"Not at the moment, captain."

"All right. But hurry! We're leaving."

The peasant opened his bag, examined the contents, and closed it again so deftly that no one noticed him slip some new cigars in among the foreign ones. With that, he shouldered his load, and the troop, following San Carlos's orders, followed him along winding, labyrinthine paths. The captain resumed his conversation with the peasant.

"Are you heading for the lakes?" asked the stranger.

"No," replied San Carlos, "I want to play a trick of my own on Dubois. I'm just going to make a detour around to the valley of Argelès and from there I'll cut across to Catarave."

"What about the detachment at Fourmont?"

"It's blind and deaf."

"I'd rather take a chance on going by the lakes. The customs officers have no boat. You come up on the opposite shore and before they can get around the merchandise is safe and sound in the Geret woods.

"Well, old chap," said San Carlos. "You certainly know the region. But what's the point of all these precautions? I've got some accomplices in the customs who'll make sure they don't stop me from getting through."

The peasant shrugged. "Let's go, then," he said.

San Carlos looked at him closely. "What do you say?"

"I say it's impossible."

"Well, you should know, since you know everything. By the way, why don't you make a clean break and become a smuggler?"

"I don't like shooting."

"But what would you do if we had to shoot it out?"

"I'd fall flat on the ground."

"You're a bigger coward than most people. I told you that before."

By now the band had come to a main road that was a little less rocky than the rough paths they had been walking on so far. A few plants timidly pushed their pretty heads up among the stones, wherever there was room, keeping their lovely eyes closed until morning. The fluttering plumes of the long-leafed saxifrage slumped mournfully to the ground, forgetting, as they slept, their nearby rivals, the purple thistle and the spiny-leafed acanthus. Various species of heather intermingled their silent stalks here and there. The rhododendrons had extinguished the countless rays of light which, in the bright sunshine, call forth brilliant colors from their fertile blossoms. The white lilies had mysteriously closed the lobes of their satin calyxes and were waiting in silence for daybreak before addressing to heaven their dazzling prayers and perfumed hymns, in harmony with bird songs and human prayers of thanksgiving.

But over all this climbing loveliness spread a heavy, black night, supremely indifferent to the beauties it was concealing and to the rays of light snuffed out by its darkness. It was not ashamed of the Hottentot shades and the Abyssinian colors in which the newest creations concealed themselves. But Captain San Carlos's men paid no attention to them either, and when they reached the road they did not notice how the vegetation had changed. They did not know where their leader was taking them, and not one of them could have given the true latitude of this unknown region.

San Carlos was following his plan. He had purposely taken extra detours on the way in order the check out a few suspicions, and now he was returning to the Cauterets road, which they had already traveled, to get to Lake Gaube.

"Now then, my friend," he said to the peasant.

"Captain?"

"Where are we?"

"You're asking me where we are?" said the astonished peasant.

"Yes. What road is this?"

"It's the main road to Argelès."

"Good. You know your geography all right. It's lucky for me that I met you. Without you, I'd have got lost in these tangled labyrinths. Thanks!"

"Well then, captain, since we're almost there, I'll take my leave."

"Oh no, you won't."

"Why not?"

"I'll tell you why, my friend. Because two of my men are going to keep an eye on you."

The peasant was taken by surprise. "On me?" he asked.

"Yes, on you. Because this is not the road to Argelès. It's the road to Cauterets. We went along here about an hour ago. So then, either you're from around here or you aren't. If you are, you deliberately deceived me and led me astray. If you aren't, then you deceived me by telling me that you were a native and a friend of Captain Urbano. Either way, you're a liar, and around here a liar means a spy. I could smash your head, but I won't."

The peasant made no reply. He took his place at the back of the line, between two smugglers, who guarded him closely. San Carlos paid no more attention to him. Hurrying his comrades along and leaving the Arastille lakes on the horizon to his left, he headed for Lake Gaube.

Mount Vignemale could already be seen rising out of the clear water, half an hour's march away. The captain set out again over terrain rarely trodden by the foot of man. His exhausting march was often interrupted by granite walls that had to be scaled at the cost of injuries to hands and knees. The few shallow streams were easy to ford. None of the smugglers complained about the long journey or the rough path.

Captain San Carlos wanted to put that nearly inaccessible expanse of water between him and his pursuers. He was hoping to find the ferry that only he knew about, and which old Cornedoux reserved for his most adventurous expeditions. The customs agents would have trouble following him and soon he would reach the dark, dense woods, where his tracks would easily be lost. Everything had to be taken into account – and it was. What if Cornedoux were not there? What if the ferry had been destroyed? San Carlos headed for the Pic d'Estour and deposited his contraband in safe hiding places marked out in advance. The vagueness of Jacopo's reports left him in the unpleasant situation of having to decide whether to turn left or right to go around the lake. As for spies among the customs officers, he had not a single one. He had boasted about his outside help only to frighten the traitor who had come amongst them.

The smugglers had been heading northwest for some time now, walking more silently than the legendary ghosts. The danger increased as they approached the lake. Death-dealing bullets might attack the little band from every crack in the rocks. From behind every boulder might come a flash of light and a deadly rain. They kept their eyes and ears open and their guns in their hands, but their hearts were strong and there was no quickening heartbeat to betray an unlikely panic or an unknown terror. The smugglers walked single file along the narrow paths, with San Carlos in the lead. The peasant was in the rear, closely

Lake Gaube in the Pyrenees, France, 1890.

watched by two men. Apparently unconcerned, he was calmly smoking an excellent *tercena* that he had taken from his pocket.

"Would you like to try one?" he asked his guards.

It was an offer not to be refused,

The peasant let them take their pick from the bag he had just bought and soon they were puffing on two fine *prensados*. But in a few moments their heads grew heavy, their legs gave way under them, their eyes closed in spite of them, and they called for help to the others, who had been too busy to notice anything. Hearing their cries, their comrades turned around, and in an instant San Carlos was beside them.

"What's the matter? What's wrong with you?"

Long yawns were the only reply, and the two men fell to the ground, dead to the world.

"Where's the peasant?"

They looked around. There was no one there. He had drugged his guards with opium-treated cigars and then run away.

"Let's get going," shouted San Carlos. "They'll wake up tomorrow. We haven't a minute to lose, friends. The enemy is on our trail already, and your lives depend on your speed. In a quarter of an hour we'll be at the lake and the customs boys have no boat to follow us. So let's be off, and woe betide anyone who doesn't keep up!"

The captain picked up the bags dropped by the two sleeping guards and turned onto a side path, followed by his eight men. The night grew darker than ever, and Mount Vignemale stood out with its impossibly steep escarpments. San Carlos knew where there was a cleft between two perpendicular cones of rock and headed into it without hesitation, even though one man with a machine gun, between them and the lake, could easily have wiped out the entire band. The smugglers threaded their way through the thick darkness, holding out their hands to avoid bumping into sharp projections of rock and sometimes crawling under an overhanging rock on their hands and knees. They looked like a long snake gliding noiselessly through a crack in an old stone wall.

At the end of that grueling pass lay Lake Gaube, where the customs officers were no doubt awaiting the inevitable arrival of their prey. But San Carlos was counting on their ignorance of the general area and of this rock in particular. Once he and his men reached the shore, they would be only a hundred paces from the old ferryman's cabin, and his boat would take them to safety.

But was there a ferry? Was the boatman there? Would their group not be decimated by the customs men?

As he neared the opposite end, San Carlos went ahead by himself, crawling so carefully that his movements would not have betrayed him to the most attentive ear. Once outside the opening, he raised his head and saw nothing. He slipped down to the bank. Nothing there. He was heading for the cabin when he noticed a man standing motionless beside the lake. He crept up to him unseen, put one arm around his body and the other hand over his mouth.

"Oh my God!" said the stranger.

"Cornedoux!" said San Carlos.

"San Carlos," said Cornedoux. "What the hell?"

"Sh! We're surrounded."

"Yes. The customs men are prowling all around."

"What about your boat? Is it still in good shape?"

"It's ready."

"Cast off and bring it up to the shore near the opening."

"Right, captain."

San Carlos went back to his men and signaled for them to come out. They got to him just as the boat reached the shore, and he and his eight men got in. The ferryman stayed on shore and the smugglers headed out into the open water.

"We're safe!" said the captain. "Row hard!"

Lake Gaube is not much more than a league an a half in circumference. In places it is twenty or twenty-five fathoms deep.[11] A number of streams, tiny tributaries of the Gave, flow into it. It is about a league from the Pont d'Espagne, which spans one of its tributaries, and about two leagues from Cauterets and Catarave.

The boat the smugglers were using was of a bizarre design, with bulges at the bow and stern, and could make only a moderate speed. The tobacco, guns, and powder had been placed in large oak boxes, copper-lined and completely waterproof. If the barge should happen to sink, the merchandise would not be damaged. These special boxes, big enough to hold items on which duty would be charged, were smuggled through by the wily smugglers. Woolens, leather goods, hides, handkerchiefs, ham, butter, fine wines, textiles, oil, tobacco, dyes, soap, and metals were concealed in them on a daily basis and made their way to

---

11. A fathom is equal to six feet.

From *Mathias Sandorf* (1885).

secret trading posts in the frontier towns.

The eight men rowed in silence, with San Carlos guiding the boat. They moved slowly across the still water, which gave no help whatsoever to the efforts of the rowers. But San Carlos knew that one branch of the Gave was fed by the lake itself, and created an underwater current before leaving the lake. He intended to take advantage of it.

Suddenly they heard the unexpected sound of oars beating irregularly on the water.

"What's that?" asked the smugglers in a low voice.

"Sh!" said San Carlos.

The visibility was five paces at the most.

"Ahoy! You in the boat!" cried a voice with a French accent.

"They've caught us!" said San Carlos. Trusting to his memory, he steered the boat more quickly towards the current that he believed was there.

"Each of you," said San Carlos to his men, "tie one of these ropes around your chest."

The ropes were about ten fathoms long, and attached to the boat's gunwales.

"Ahoy! Fire!"

The lake suddenly lit up, and San Carlos saw that he was surrounded by four boats filled with customs officers. Among them, shouting out orders, was the peasant who had escaped. San Carlos recognized him; it was François Dubuc.

"I've got you now, San Carlos!" shouted the sergeant.

"Not yet, my friend," replied the captain.

"Forward," shouted the sergeant.

"Dive!" shouted the captain.

The rowboats were now only a few feet away from the smugglers' boat. They rushed towards it. The impact would surely shatter it to bits. But to the officers' amazement, it was their own boats that collided with one another. San Carlos, his men, and his ferry, had all disappeared.

"They've been annihilated," said the officers.

"That's odd," said François Dubuc. "They've gone down with all hands." The boats traveled back and forth across the scene of the disaster.

"Nothing," said the sergeant. "Not a scrap of wreckage. Not a body."

They searched for a quarter of an hour, but in vain. He saw nothing. He found nothing. A torch was lit, and at that moment the agents could see the smugglers climbing the hill on the opposite side of the lake, carrying their bundles. It was so uncanny that they nearly choked with rage.

The fact is that the sergeant knew nothing about those mysterious boats with air chambers in the bow and stern that kept them at a constant depth when they submerged. When he was on the point of being smashed into a thousand pieces, San Carlos had opened a valve in the bottom of the boat, submerging it to a depth of about ten fathoms. The underwater current had soon carried it to the nearby shore, towing

Pont d'Espagne, upper falls, Cauterets, Pyrenees, France, 1890.

behind it the men attached to its gunwales, who had then pulled it up onto the bank. The smugglers had taken the merchandise, guns, and powder out of the chests and were now striding across the fields that lay between them and the Geret woods, escaping before the astonished eyes of the dumfounded customs offices.

"Fire!" shouted the sergeant, but the bullets went wide of their mark.

Dubois was beside himself. "Come on, lads," he cried, and the boats flew across the surface of the lake to the cove where Captain San Carlos and his men had just gone ashore. But the mysterious boat had been sent back to its watery habitat, where the old ferryman found it later and easily hid it from the prying eyes of the well-paid employees of the revenue department.

With loaded rifles, the customs men stepped ashore and hurriedly set out on the trail of their enemies. But the smugglers had a head start and were running away at a brisk pace, despite their heavy loads. Nevertheless, every time San Carlos came to a little height of land, he looked back and saw that his pursuers were gaining on him. The customs men kept firing from time to time, their bullets landing at the very feet of the exhausted smugglers.

And so they reached the Pont d'Espagne, a structure made of fir trunks twenty-five or thirty feet long, spanning the Gave River and supported by enormous blocks of granite some forty feet high. San Carlos saw that his men were dead tired and that the customs officers were about to catch up with them. But once they had crossed the bridge, he darted behind one of the rocks at the foot of the magnificent Gave waterfall and clambered down its vertical face with amazing skill. The smugglers followed him and made their way along a path – which was really only a rock ledge a foot wide – to a point where they were concealed by the waterfall itself. There they found a crevasse in which they hastily tossed their merchandise, and scattered in all directions.

When the customs officers came to the bridge they hurried across it, but since they saw and heard nothing, they went back the way they had come. They scoured the area for hours, but the only satisfaction they got was that of telling each other to go to the devil (who has little use for people of that sort).

The sacks of tobacco arrived at Catarave the next day on the backs of hand-picked men, who had been dispatched to the crevasse at the Pont d'Espagne by the town's merchants. San Carlos and his men got the price they had bargained for and headed back to the mountains, singing their cheeriest songs and swearing by all the saints in their calendar that smugglers were, and always would be, the happiest people in the world, as long as there were cigars in Spain and green-jackets trying to keep them out of France.

✠

FUTURE OF THE SUBMARINE

The following article by Jules Verne first appeared in the June 1904 issue of Popular Mechanics, *and this is its first complete appearance in book form, revealing Verne's more mature thinking on the subject. Since "San Carlos" was not published during Verne's lifetime, his readers would not have known of the story, and he only mentions Captain Nemo's* Nautilus *of* Vingt Mille Lieues sous les mers *(Twenty Thousand Leagues Under the Seas, 1870). However, Verne also neglects to mention here his novel,* Face au drapeau *(Facing the Flag, 1896), in which a submarine becomes part of the arsenal of an international outlaw, and even an underwater battle between submarines occurs. So, too, Verne imagined beyond a submarine in* Maître du monde *(Master of the World, 1904) to a single vehicle that could travel on and below the ocean, on land and fly through the air. The final thoughts expressed in this article offer the evolution of Verne's reflections about the submarine.*

FOR SOME INEXPLICABLE REASON many people insist upon regarding me as the inventor, or the imaginer, of the submarine. I am not in any way the inventor of submarine navigation, and reference to the authorities will show that many years—fully fifty, I should say, before I wrote about the *Nautilus*—the Italians were at work upon submarine war vessels, and other nations were busied with them, too. All that I did was to avail myself of the great privileges of the fiction writer, spring over every scientific difficulty with fancy's seven-leagued boots, and create on paper what other men were planning out in steel and other metals.

The future of the submarine, as I regard it—and let me here disclaim all gift of prophecy—is to be wholly a war future. The *Nautilus*, as I have written of it, will never be, I think, an actual fact, and I do not believe that under-sea ships will be built in future years to carry traffic across the ocean's bed to America and to Australia. Even if the air difficulty were successfully encountered (and I have my grave doubts as to the possibility of that), what would be gained by any such sub-ocean traffic except freedom from sea-sickness? No submarine would ever cross the bed of the Atlantic faster than a ship upon the waves would traverse it, and surely freedom from that bugbear is not a sufficient incentive for the creation of a Cunard line beneath the sea.

I am an old man now, and working, as well as my deficient eyesight will allow me, upon my one hundred and second volume of boys' stories and as I look back on the years which have passed since I first wrote the life-story of the *Nautilus*, and of its owner, I see no progress in the submarine which makes me hope for its use as a commercial medium. It has been wonderfully improved, I grant you—miraculously improved

Two submarines prepare for battle in *Face au drapeau* (*Facing the Flag*, 1896).

almost—but the improvements have all tended to one point—its efficacy as a war weapon; and that will be its one use in the future, I believe. I even think that in the distant future the submarine may be the cause of bringing battle to a stoppage altogether, for fleets will become useless, and as other war material continues to improve, war will become impossible. As time goes on, each nation will acquire a large and very rapid fleet of submarines. Each little vessel (I am inclined to think that in the future they will be smaller than they are today, and manned by one or two men only) will be absolutely in control, and will be able with scientific accuracy to place torpedoes underneath the greatest vessels, and to blow those vessels up. I do not think that any apparatus will be found to counteract the intense rapidity and certainty of the submarine, and eventually, when every nation has its fleet of hundreds of these little vessels, what is to war with them? They may be able even to blow up huge tracts of country, and retreat unseen, some day; who knows?

Of course, before these things can be, improvements in the submarine will have to be manifold, and almost as wonderfully ingenious as the beginnings of this greatest wonder of man's science; but these things will, I think, be possible.

I followed very carefully the experiments made lately during the French maneuvers in the Mediterranean, and during the maneuvers of the English fleet, and I was very much struck by the accuracy with which the submarines of both fleets managed to slip in, strike, and get away in safety.

Imagine hundreds of these vessels with their deadly freight. Can you suggest that any means would counteract their deadly power? I do not think so. The refraction of the water, the depths to which the submarine can sink, its freedom from all observation—all these things make it the deadliest of war inventions, and in future years, when I myself am under ground, these powers will be enhanced. I do not think that apparatus will be found to render them more harmless. The sea is hard to pierce, and I can think of nothing, even upon paper, which will enable men on board the supermare vessels to trace the tracks of their deadly little foes beneath the waves.

But as a commercial item in the world's civilization, I do not think that submarines have any future. Air may be found for them, but even so it will never be found plentifully enough to make it possible for a large number of passengers to travel for a length of time in comfort. Electricity for their propulsion may, one day, be gathered from the sea itself, but

I have doubts of it; and even if these things were done, the pressure of the sea at any depth would crush a submarine to fragments unless some hitherto unheard-of metal were discovered which would withstand the pressure. Think of the size a trans-Atlantic submarine would have to be, and think how slowly it must travel, owing to the pressure of the waters round it, and tell me if you think a Majestic will ever be made to travel to New York upon the sea bottom.

I doubt it—doubt it very gravely; and, as I have said, I do not see that there is any need for submarine trans-ocean vessels. But submarine fleets are in the near future and they will, I believe, prove the thin end of the beneficent wedge which will cause war to cease between the nations, owing to their very deadliness. Unfortunately their work will not be done in my time. I am a man of peace and should have loved to see it, but it seems that my fading eyes are destined to behold sickening carnage in the unequal contest of the improved submarine machine with the heavy battleship, whose days are numbered.

✠

THE SIEGE OF ROME

Translated by Edward Baxter

Chapter I

HISTORICAL BACKGROUND

THE ASSASSINATION OF MR. ROSSI would prove to be the prelude to the revolutionary movements in Italy.[1] The liberties that Pius IX had proclaimed would turn against him and overthrow for some time the ancient throne of Saint Peter.[2]

If the liberal powers were falling on all sides, it was because of the very excess of their institutions. Long ago is very far away from the present day. In the past, when absolute governments attacked public liberties and overthrew them, those liberties, like bombs, exploded as they fell, but in the nineteenth century, the people themselves call for restrictions on the overly liberal reforms that could plunge them into a bottomless abyss. Liberty, as understood by various Republicans, anarchistic liberty, has had its day. Liberty in principle and liberty in fact are mutually exclusive. Wherever the principle is proclaimed aloud, the fact no longer exists. Hence, the principle has no reason to be inscribed on the front of public buildings when the free exercise of liberty has inevitably been lost.[3]

---

1. Pellegrino Rossi, born in Carrare in 1787, was a respected Catholic and liberal jurist. The head of the pontifical government, he was assassinated on November 15, 1848.

2. Pope Pius IX, born in 1792, succeeded Gregory XVI in 1846. He was thought to be somewhat sympathetic to the liberal and nationalist movements in Italy, initially winning the support of Garibaldi and Mazzini. After 1849, Pius IX refused to introduce any reforms to the Papal State. He died in 1878.

3. For similar political views, see also the beginning of chapter 5 in the present novelette, as well as the presentation in more detailed form in Verne's novel *Magellania*, rewritten by Michel Verne as *Les Naufragés du Jonathan* (*The Survivors of the Jonathan*, 1909).

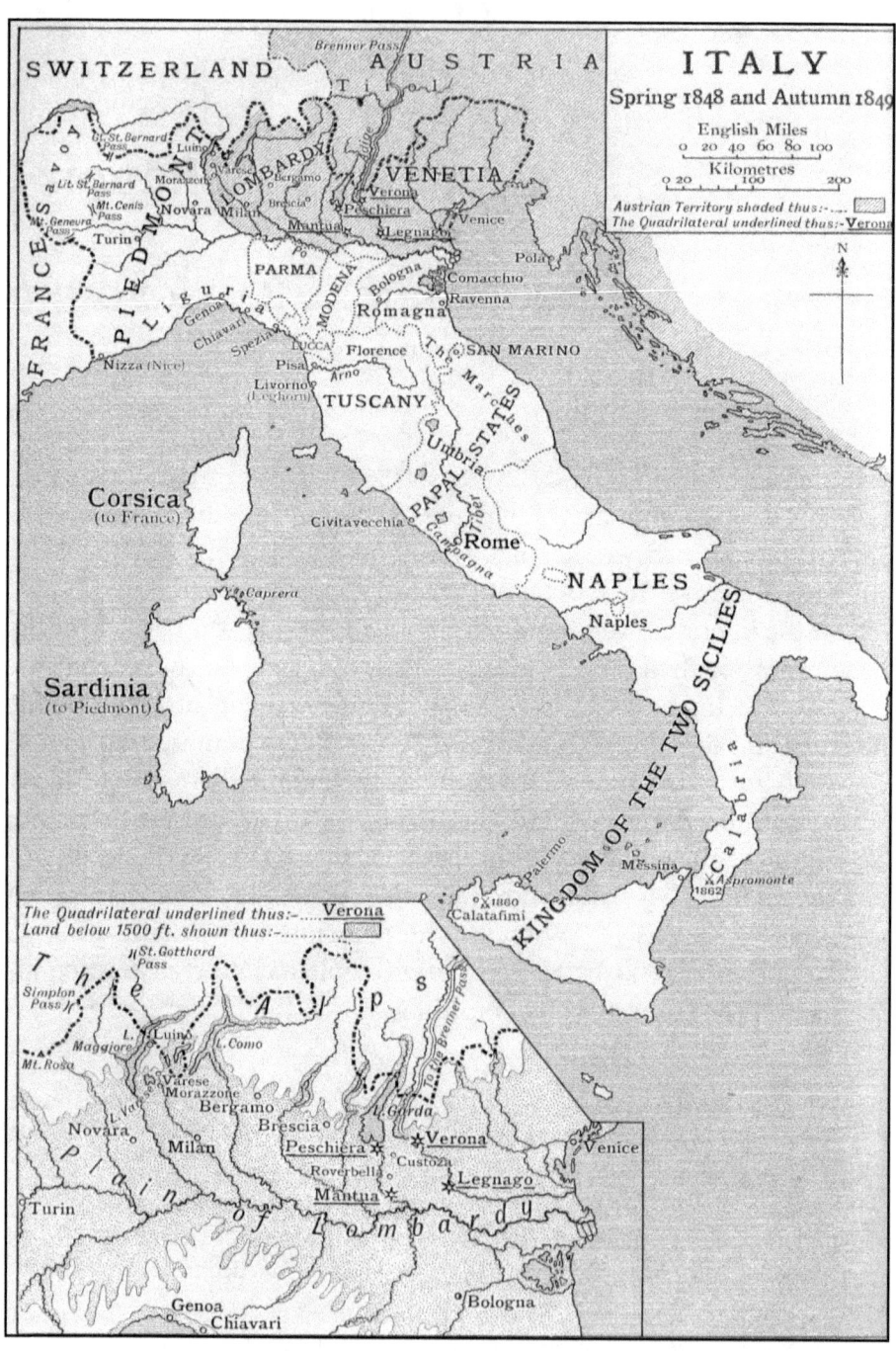

ITALY
Spring 1848 and Autumn 1849

On November 16, 1848, the Quirinal, the palace of the sovereign pontiff, was surrounded by municipal guards and regular soldiers, but their cries for reform were greeted with gunfire by the Swiss, who, ever loyal to power and to the money it pays, bravely defended the temporal authority of the pope.

For some time, the air in Rome had been sinister and turbulent. France had sent a little of its atmosphere to Italy, and chests in the Peninsula were inhaling deep breaths of that intoxicating breeze. But the Italians can hardly breathe without permission from the emperor of Austria, and there is very little in the way of generosity to be found in cannons and generals.[4] And so the Romans, excited by all the noise they were hearing from beyond the Alps, wanted to be in on the party, and treat themselves unceremoniously to the spectacle of a little revolution.

While the attackers and the attacked were fighting it out around the Quirinal, a young man with a mean and evil face, Andreani Corsetti, was busily mingling with the crowds milling about the square. He was one of those false, hypocritical Italians, inured to evil, impervious to good, living on that ultramontane nature that is so low, so groveling, so envious, so cowardly, so treacherous, when it has not been directed and raised up by study or reason. A former lay secretary to Pius IX, he was well known in society, on whose heads he had long ago let fall his haughtiness and insolence. His former rank was bound to cast suspicion on his current occupation. Why was Andreani abandoning the pope's cause to become involved in riot and insurrection?

"My friends, my brothers," he shouted in the midst of the over-wrought crowd, "the temporal power of the popes is on its death-bed, and a free Italy will not go into mourning for those tyrants. Let us emulate the enthusiasm and liberty of France, and its children will come flocking to our aid."

"But you aren't one of us," people said to him.

"I am a soldier. I am with you and for you. I have seen at first hand the countless abuses of that dethroned royalty, the so-called reforms with which they distracted you in your impatience, and the empty concessions, which are only counterfeit money to pay for your generous aspirations. I am a soldier. You will find me fighting in the front ranks to overthrow absolutism and ensure your independence forever."

---

4.   At the time, Italy consisted of several separate states, many dominated by foreign powers.

"Surely you must know what is going on in the palace," replied an honest moderate. "You must know that Pius IX is acceding to our wishes by giving us a liberal minister."

"Ministers are passive instruments of power, and do not change its policy in the least," replied Andreani, who was becoming more and more excited. "The pope is putting on new gloves, that's all. His hand will be no gentler and no more charitable. Have nothing to do with those temporary names, with which power attempts to countersign its arbitrary acts. What difference does a new sign make, if the master still gives his clients short weight when he sells his counterfeit liberties?"

Indeed, the sovereign pontiff, in order to fend off the storm, had tried to use these ministers as lightning rods, to deflect the thunderbolts and render them harmless. But all those dull and rusty names were no longer enough to protect the papal throne. The streets of Rome were filling up with outbursts of anger, which led to gunfire around the Quirinal. The troops were siding with the rebels and fighting alongside them. For a week Pius IX hoped to put down the revolt by skillful moves and timely reforms, because he thought it was just an ordinary uprising. Riots have safety valves that can be opened in time to let the popular ferment escape, but revolutions do not. This was a revolution, and it burst out.

On November 24, 1848, followed by his cardinals, princes of the Church, and by some of the clergy, the pope hurriedly left Rome. For several days, it was not known where His Holiness had taken refuge. A supreme junta was appointed to replace the executive power temporarily and to form a cabinet, which was soon complete.

However, the pope, whom no one had bothered in the least during his flight, had withdrawn to Gaeta, from where, on December 17, he issued a protest against the supreme junta.[5] He had not fled from his states in order to yield to the revolution and give it a free hand. His Holiness considered himself more clearly destined for martyrdom than that. But it was important that the pope should keep his independence intact. Indeed, the Catholic world might have believed, under the circumstances, that he was no longer free to exercise his spiritual power.

The protest was legally sound, but in fact it accomplished nothing, and the junta carried on regardless. The pope himself was really no longer to be feared, but many defenders would soon rally to his standard.

---

5.   Gaeta was in Neapolitan territory. Pius IX escaped the pressures of the new government established in Rome by the revolution.

Pope Pius IX in 1866.

Several plans for intervention were mulled over here and there. That was why, on December 2, it was the turn of the Roman government to take a stand against the expedition ordered by General Cavaignac, head of the executive power in France at that time. But mediation by the French was not an accomplished fact.

Social movements have the sorry privilege of bringing all the obscure and putrid dregs to the surface. For every man of true worth who emerges from the conflict of events, there are a hundred mediocre or incompetent ones. Consequently, everyone who possesses any half-formed ambition, any feverish and impossible utopia, any shameful and outraged misery, any overflowing hatred in his heart, any hidden premeditated revenge, considers himself called upon to decide the destinies of nations. Those people must be deaf not to hear the voice of private interest, which, for them, drowns out the voice of public interest. Andreani was totally deaf in that respect, and since a total absence of principles reduced his specific and moral weight to almost zero, he rose rapidly to the surface of the disturbance. How far he had come from his greetings and contrite genuflections of the past! He had become a turncoat, and that did not change him at all, because his coat was dirty both inside and out.

General Cavaignac.

After the pope left, he flung himself body and soul into the revolution and cheered lustily in favor of liberty, although his own heart and conscience were bound up with treason and malice. And so, when Garibaldi first appeared on the political scene, he rushed to take his place under the flag of that bold adventurer.[6] He accepted a commission in the ranks of that daring legion and used some of his hatred to inflame Pius IX's enemies.

No one had been surprised by this desertion, instances of which had already been seen among members of the clergy. In a country where titles rain down in torrents, where princes proliferate and nobles abound, the lower classes of the clergy are reduced to the most abject servitude. The loosening of moral standards is less pronounced at the bottom than at the top. It is not poverty alone that rules out loose living on the part of the lower clergy; it is poverty subjected to hierarchical despotism. While the princes of the Church, the cardinals, cloak the shameful practices of their private lives in mystery, they condemn to a life of virtue the priests of a lower order, who have at their disposal neither villas, nor palaces, nor lackeys, nor thugs to serve, exploit, and hide their disorderly conduct. As a result, the great lords appear to be what they are not, and do not appear to be what they are, while the simple ministers of religion, who have no wish

---

6. Giuseppe Garibaldi (1807-1882), is considered both an Italian hero and a revered independent international military figure and statesman celebrated in both Europe and South America. His courage and military audacity are legendary, and his popularity, skill in rousing the common people, and military exploits not only helped make the unification of Italy possible, but made him a global exemplar of mid-19th century revolutionary nationalism and liberalism.

   In Geneva in 1833, Garibaldi met Giuseppe Mazzini, and joined the Carbonari revolutionary association, fleeing Italy after a failed insurrection. Living in Uruguay and Brazil, he adopted his trademark clothing, which consisted of the red shirt, poncho, and sombrero commonly worn by the gauchos. At Mazzini's urging, in 1849, Garibaldi, only back in Italy for a year, took command of the defence of Rome. In April 30, the Republican army, under Garibaldi's command, defeated a numerically far superior French army. Subsequently, French reinforcements arrived, and the siege of Rome began on June 1. After a truce on July 1, Garibaldi withdrew from Rome with 4,000 followers, but after an epic march pusued by Austrian, French, Spanish, and Neapolitan troops, he reached San Marino with only 250 men still following him; his wife, carrying their fifth child, had died on the retreat. In later years he again marched upon Rome, and sought international support for altogether eliminating the papacy. With the French Third Republic, he went to France and assumed command of the Army of the Vosges, an army of volunteers that was never defeated by the Prussians.

to be poor by reason of virtue, are necessarily virtuous by reason of poverty.

Andreani, the proletarian, felt passion tormenting his heart, but why, after having risen, through ambition and skill, to a position of confidence in the pontifical government, was he cast down one day among the plebeians?

That was something that neither his friends nor his enemies could ever find out. One morning he was abruptly handed his dismissal notice and exiled from the Vatican, without any reason for his downfall having ever come to light. He was one of the Holy Father's personal servants, and Pius IX, a just man, eminently pious and rigorously dogmatic, who had formerly used his indestructible honor in the interests of France, had no doubt considered the secretary Andreani to be less than honorable. What odious action had exposed the soul of this evil man? No one knows. At that time, vague rumors of breach of trust and abduction circulated throughout the city. The question was never clarified. The crime (if there was a crime) must not have been committed in Rome, and when Andreani was removed from his post, he had only recently returned from France, where the pope had sent him on a special mission.

And, since he had visited France, how greatly he had admired the inimitable purity of the French clergy! What dignity! What nobility, compared with the abuses of power, the injustices, and the widespread shameless acts of the princes of the Church! While the latter used their religious influence to further their passions, the former suppressed their passions in asceticism to strengthen that influence. While French clergymen practice the virtue that they preach, the noble cardinals abduct and seduce young children who come on bended knee to beg forgiveness for their peccadillos. And while those wealthy prelates force some honest cavalier to use his honor to conceal the dishonoring of their victim, the French priests devote their lives to every misfortune, bestow their blessings on all human endeavors, and offer their condolences in the presence of all suffering. During their arduous ministry, without rest, without joy, without pleasure, they spend their nights praying for the unfortunate ones to whom they have dedicated their days.

Andreani had smiled with pity at these acts of devotion, so often unclear and misunderstood. At the time of his downfall, he said aloud, "The ways of the Lord are inscrutable. Blessed be his holy name." And

Garibaldi in 1849.

under his breath he said, "Popes and cardinals will pass away." And so he devoted himself body and soul to the shady machinations of the Republican Party and participated actively in the movement of the insurgents, who, on November 16, 1848, aimed their cannons at the gates of the Quirinal.

What could Pius IX do when his enemies included people who knew neither law nor honor? It saddened him to see the ranks of honest Republicans sullied by the presence of such men. Why then do these humanitarian armies become protected zones, where criminals hope to hide from the law? These alliances destroy the tact and delicacy of parties. When the pope, lacking any means of repression, rightfully excommunicated anyone who committed the sin of attacking the temporal sovereignty of the Holy See, cries of "Long live the excommunicated!" rang out through all the streets of Rome. In the past, people trembled when the sovereign pontiff unleashed his thunderbolts, thinking they were being thrown by the hand of God. Today, mockery has made them ridiculous. Godless physics has made tremendous progress; consciences are now equipped with lightning rods.

Despite these excommunications, the junta continued its work. Universal suffrage brought votes from all the Papal States. Through negligence, carelessness, or premeditation on the part of the scrutineers, many foreigners, who had neither homeland nor place of residence, came and cast their cosmopolitan affiliation into the ballot box. But these makers of governments cannot take the time to be scrupulous. Justly or unjustly, a republic was proclaimed at Rome on Febru-

Giuseppe Mazzini.

ary 9, 1849. The temporal power of the popes was abolished, but their spiritual power was still guaranteed. The idiots did not understand that religion, in order to be strong, had to be independent, and that its independence resided in the temporal authority of its supreme leader, because that prevented it from becoming subject to the laws and the will of a foreign nation. The new government would have whatever relations with Italy were required by a common nationality. While the pope was gathering his most faithful followers together at Gaeta, the Constituent Assembly was hailing Mazzini, the king of the republicans of central Italy, with enthusiastic cheers.[7]

And to celebrate this lovely day of Italian independence, the great hymn of victory, sung until then only by ministers of heaven, but now shouted out with savage fury, the hymn of the God of armies, the "Te Deum," burst forth in the Vatican.

---

7. Giuseppi Mazzini (1805-1872) was an Italian politician, journalist and activist for the unification of Italy and the modern European movement for popular democracy in a Republican state, expanding the tradition of the French Revolution. He hoped that in the distant future free nations might combine to form a loosely federal Europe with some kind of federal assembly. Mazzini participated in uprisings and was exiled several times.

Chapter II

THE TRUCE

THE QUESTION OF INTERVENTION in the affairs of Rome was then referred to the French National Assembly. In principle, the motion put forward was only a request for twelve thousand men to be sent to Italy to occupy a position against Austria. This plan was so vague that it was bound to attain gigantic proportions later on, and it turned out that the Eternal City became the important position at which the French army would encamp.

The plan for intervention was adopted by the Chamber and the expeditionary force was soon mobilized. Duke Oudinot de Reggio was named commander-in-chief and Regnault Saint-Jean-d'Angély, general of the troops.[1] This duplication of commands went against

---

1. Lieutenant-General Charles Nicolas Victor Oudinot, 2nd Duc de Reggio (1791-1863) was the eldest son by the first marriage of Nicolas Charles Oudinot, 1st Comte Oudinot, 1st Duc de Reggio, a Marshal of France under Napoleon I. (The Marshal of France is a military distinction, not a rank, granted to generals for exceptional achievements; during the First French Empire the title was "Marshal of the Empire".) The younger Oudinot also undertook a military career, and served through the later campaigns of Napoleon, 1809–1814, but unlike his father was a cavalryman. He wrote a memoir of his re-establishment of the temporal power of Pope Pius IX. Oudinot supported the resistance of the Second Republic against Louis Napoleon's coup d'état of December 2, 1851, after which he retired from military and political life, although remaining in Paris.

   Auguste Michel Etienne Comte Regnaud de Saint-Jean d'Angély (1794-1870), later 2nd Comte Regnaud de Saint-Jean d'Angély, was a soldier and politician. Trained at Saint-Cyr, a veteran of the 1812 campaign in Russia, he served as an orderly to Emperor Napoleon I until the defeat at Waterloo. Dismissed from the army by the Restoration government, in 1825 he went to Greece and fought in the war of independence (the setting of Verne's *L'Archipel en feu* (*The*

all the rules. The appointment of the Duke de Reggio under these circumstances was not in keeping with the usual custom and was, hierarchically speaking, illogical. At least two divisions must be combined under the orders of a commander-in-chief, but there was only one, and General Regnault Saint-Jean-d'Angély could have commanded it himself.

The army corps consisted of the 1st infantry battalion and six regiments of the line, two under the orders of Brigadier-General Mollière, two commanded by Brigadier-General Levaillant, and two led by Brigadier-General Chadeysson.[2] Three batteries of artillery, two companies of engineers, and two squadrons from the 1st cavalry regiment completed the expeditionary force.

This task force of six thousand five hundred men soon set sail and came within sight of Civitavecchia on April 24, 1849. The commander-in-chief did not know what the mood of the populace was, but it was important that the landing should be made at that point, or else the squadron would have had to anchor at the little port of Fiumicino, at the mouth of the Tiber, with its dangerous deposits of silt. The Duke de Reggio was soon aware that a hundred and twenty cannons were lined up on the shore at Civita, making a friendly reception appear unlikely. He therefore wrote and had posted in the city a proclamation declaring that the French army was coming as a friend, and was not about to impose on the people a government that would not have their sympathy.

While waiting for the time to drop anchor, two young men were chatting aboard the *Labrador*. One of them was a young staff captain who was not officially part of the Rome expedition, but had obtained permission to accompany the campaign as an observer. His request,

---

Archipelago on Fire, 1884). In 1852, he backed Louis-Napoléon Bonaparte and, as a reward, he was made a senator for life. Although his father's illegitmate son, and unable to inherit his title, it was granted by Napoleon III in 1864. Under the Second Empire, he went through the Crimean and Italian campaigns, and ultimately was named Marshal of France in 1859 for bravery at the Battle of Magenta.

2. Jean Levaillant (1794-1871) won many decorations in a military career that began in 1811 and took him afield to campaigns in Spain and Africa before serving in the expedition to Rome. He was made a Marshal of France in 1851, minister of war in 1854, and commander-in-chief of the Army in Italy in 1859.

supported by a high-ranking person who was no doubt aware of the secret reasons for it, was taken under consideration and granted. He was a sad and worried young man named Henri Formont. What endless and distressing sorrows must have intruded on his early years, since he wept at an age when one does not yet know how to weep! He was accompanied and watched over by a kind and valiant comrade, Lieutenant Annibal de Vergennes of the engineers, whose lively and exuberant cheerfulness contrasted with the gloomy thoughts of the young captain.

"Do you think," said Henri, "that we'll get ashore at Civitavecchia without meeting any opposition?"

"I certainly hope not," replied the lieutenant distractedly.

"That's too bad, because I wouldn't want to get killed at the beginning of this campaign."

"Be careful, then, my dear Henri, because usually observers don't get back home. There are bullets with their names on them."

"Oh! Just let them spare me until I get to Rome," said Henri Formont darkly.

Annibal gripped his hand with deep affection.

"My friend, you don't want to tell me why you're so sad. That's a mistake. It shows a lack of confidence. My heart and my arm are at your service. If, as I suspect, you want to get revenge on someone you hate, then bear in mind that it concerns both of us."

"My dear Annibal, my vengeance is decided on, but I still have to subordinate it to the events that will follow. Yes, I have an enemy in Rome whom I hate with all my might, and I pray heaven that he may not meet an honorable death by a bullet, because I need him alive in order to bring about his death."

"Fine," replied Annibal, "we'll take him prisoner. One of my sappers, Jean Taupin by name, is the bravest of the brave and a true Hercules, who could hold up three gabions at arm's length.[3] He'll take care of this business."

"No," said Henri, with hatred in his voice. "If this man was a prisoner, he'd get away from me. And besides, I don't know him yet."

"And you hope to meet him over there?"

"Yes."

---

3.   A gabion is a cylinder of wickerwork that can be filled with earth and used as a military defense.

Duke Oudinot de Reggio.

"Who'll point him out to you?"

"God will. In two days we'll get to Rome."

"But we won't be *in* Rome. There will be difficulties."

"You think there may be delays?"

"It's probable, even more than probable. If the Romans don't put up a stiff resistance to our entry into their city, they'll create a thousand diplomatic complications for us, and they'll keep us occupied at the gates with trivialities for a long time."

"It's fate! Oh! I just hope I have the strength and good fortune to live until then."

"Be patient, Henri, and keep your courage up," replied Annibal seriously. "As you see, we already have to use trickery to get into Civitavecchia. That may give you some idea of what's in store for us."

"But General Oudinot doesn't seem to have any doubts about an early victory."

"Well, if he often makes proclamations like that, he should at least have attached them to a cannonball and sent them through the city that way. After all, it's not a time to display courage when you feel like throwing up. Now I'm getting sea-sick again. Good-bye, my friend, I'm dying. I'll leave you my neck-guard. Ah!"

Annibal collapsed on the deck, but, fortunately for him and many of his comrades, the squadron had come close to shore and was ordered to drop anchor.

The municipal council of Civitavecchia, trusting the commander-in-chief's promises, opened its gates to the French division, and the landing was carried out without incident. The soldiers were warmly welcomed by the town, whose garrison they had first taken prisoner.

Orders of the day, more forthright and insistent than the proclamation, were immediately brought to the attention of the inhabitants. The army's reason for coming was to guarantee respect for the liberal institutions that Pope Pius IX had kindly conferred on his states. It was too late to resist. The city said not a word.

Without wasting any time, the commander-in-chief dispatched his brother at the head of a cavalry detachment to carry out a reconnaissance along the Civitavecchia road. News of the landing by the French troops had spread rapidly. The aide-de-camp was harassed, and in a skirmish one of his soldiers was taken prisoner by the Romans.

When he came back to the city to report on his observations, the commander-in-chief said simply:

"They have taken one of our men. Tomorrow we will take a thousand of theirs."

Two days later, he exchanged the garrison of Civita for one of his battalions, which had been captured at the outset of the campaign.

Leaving the 36th battalion in Civita, General Oudinot advanced on Rome by forced marches. Annibal was part of this bold expedition and Henri Formont mingled with the commander-in-chief's staff. Towards evening the army reached Palo, where it spent the night, having covered about half the distance of some twenty leagues.[4] At daybreak the troops resumed their march and soon reached the Roman outposts. They were greeted with rifle fire.

Carried away by his reckless enthusiasm, the commander-in-chief resolved to launch a *coup de main*. Although he lacked fighting equip-

---

4.   The distance between Civitavecchia and Rome is 70 kilometers or 43.5 miles.

ment and nothing was ready for an assault, he resolved to take Rome without waiting a day, and invited his officers to dine that very evening at the Minerve, one of the best hotels in the city. He ordered all the scaling ladders in the vicinity to be collected, to enable the soldiers to climb over the barricades drawn up in front of the gates.

"Axe and shield," said the huge sapper Jean Taupin. "Scaling ladders for gathering bullets! Excuse me!" Which did not keep him from rushing bravely into battle.

The road from Civitavecchia enters Rome by the Porta Fabricca, located roughly behind St. Peter's. Keeping the road on his left, the commander-in-chief appeared at the Porta Cavallegieri, which opens onto the fortified enclosure at the top of the Janiculum.[5] Cannons and rifles opened fire at the same time, but in the midst of the thick smoke the French soldiers, with their customary bravery, charged enemies whose numbers and position made them invincible. The 20th battalion fought with extraordinary valor, and if the inaccessible obstacle facing it could have been crossed, it would have got through. The Orleans infantry then began to demonstrate the matchless skill that distinguished them throughout the entire campaign. One of their number hid in the vines alongside the road and took aim at every gun-layer who appeared in a doorway as he was going up to serve the cannon. Every bullet found its mark. Protected by the high foliage, which even concealed the smoke from his gun, he stayed at his post for a long time, and brought down eight gun-layers, until he himself was felled by grapeshot from a cannon.

The French troops fought every inch of the way, but gained no ground, and not advancing during an attack is the same as retreating. Soon the Romans overwhelmed them. The officers tried in vain to rally their men, while realizing themselves that victory was impossible. Annibal and Henri met in the thick of the fray, and on many occasions the lieutenant of engineers saved the life of the staff officer, who, carried away by his courage and his hatred, was fighting hand to hand with the Roman soldiers.

At five o'clock the retreat was sounded. The regiments broke ranks and it was a veritable rout. General Oudinot tried in vain to organize the headlong flight and remained bravely under fire. His soldiers, who

---

5.   The Janiculum is one of the hills on which Rome is built. St. Peter's basilica is located nearby.

had scattered in all directions, were returning in groups of three or four, some carrying a wounded man on rifles arranged as a stretcher, some barely dragging themselves along, others almost dead, and all regretting their wasted courage and valor.

Annibal, Henri, and Jean Taupin were among the last to leave the walls of Rome. Then, guided by the sapper, who knew the way, they fell back to Castel di Guido. Annibal was furious; Henri was sad. Annibal was furious because of the defeat; Henri was sad because of the expedition's disastrously inauspicious beginning. The two men might be described as follows: Annibal was beside himself, whereas Henri was locked up inside himself, suffering in silence, while his valiant companion was exploding like a bomb.

"Lieutenant," said Jean Taupin, "we'll have to start all over again, and when you can get out of an unfortunate affair like this with one leg or two, you have no right to grumble."

"It's a disgrace for us," bellowed Annibal. "Have you counted up how many of our men have been killed or captured? My God! I'd really like to see how the general's reports will describe this disastrous day."

"Excuse me, lieutenant, we know now who we're up against, and these Romans, who are definitely not honest people, are still brave people. I can vouch for that, because I saw some of them meeting death bravely, all the same."

"Come now, Henri," replied the lieutenant, "don't be so sad. You fought like a soldier, I hope, and more than one Roman chest must have been amazed to find so much hatred at the point of your sword. Well? Do you understand what I'm saying?"

The young captain did not answer. The lieutenant's commiseration and the soldier's jokes left him without a smile or any sign of recognition. Soon all three were walking along in silence, and as night fell they reached Castel di Guido, where they rejoined the commander-in-chief.

Another part of the army had reached Maglianella, which meant that those troops, in headlong flight, had not been rallied until they were two leagues from Rome. When the roll was called, seven hundred and fifty men did not answer to their names.

Nevertheless, the defeat of April 30 was described as a reconnaissance in force, but there is reason to believe that the Austrians, camped on the other side of the city, and indeed all of Europe (which was paying close attention to what was happening in Italy) recognized it for what it was.

This reconnaissance in force, followed by a truce, brought about the beginning of negotiations, but badly needed reinforcements still arrived up to the walls of Rome. They continued to reach the expeditionary force, which now numbered thirty thousand men, until the end of the siege. The army in Italy was now established on a permanent basis. It consisted of three divisions commanded by Generals Regnault Saint-Jean-d'Angély, Rostolan, and Guesvillers, thirty battalions, eight squadrons, thirty-six pieces of field artillery, forty pieces of siege artillery, cannons, field howitzers, mortars, and six companies of engineers, including one company of mine-layers. Such were the imposing forces that so valiantly carried out the orders of General Thyri of the artillery and the magnificent plans of Lieutenant-General Vaillant of the engineers.

The Duke de Reggio was now in a logical position. He was the commander-in-chief. Officially, he had that title, and especially the honors, but unofficially he must have known that a man of high intelligence and eminent ability was ready to take his place in the expedition and, if necessary, assume command of the French troops. If he did not do so, it was probably because it was not customary to appoint a general of a specialized corps as commander-in-chief. That was why Lieutenant-General Vaillant of the engineers remained in a subordinate position but took over the direction of all the siege operations as soon as he arrived at the walls of Rome.

The army took up a position on the right bank of the Tiber. To the left, the 3rd division was in place at Monte-Mario, opposite the Vatican, fifteen hundred meters from the square, and at Mattei on the Via Portuense. The 2nd and 1st divisions, forming the center and right, occupied Santucci, the headquarters, more than two thousand meters to the south of Rome, and San Carlo, about seven hundred meters forward of Santucci. These two points were connected to the left bank of the river by a pontoon bridge built at Sasserra. The cavalry was deployed in the direction of Mattei and Santucci and the engineers bivouacked at San Carlo. There is no village around Rome, and these names designate convents or the properties of cardinals or Roman princes. The Duke de Reggio had his headquarters at Santucci and Lieutenant-General Vaillant at San Carlo.

Auguste Regnault de Saint-Jean d'Angély.

Annibal's company was living at San Carlo, a former convent, where they had found a few beds that looked somewhat soporific and had commandeered them without a word. They were at war, after all! At the beginning of the truce, the engineers spent their time constructing several thousand gabions and fascines.[6] Since the woods were some distance away, these were put together on the spot and brought to the camp with the help of the infantry and requisitioned vehicles.

---

6. A fascine is a bundle of sticks bound together, used for such tasks as lining trenches or filling ditches.

The soldiers, somewhat frustrated by the defeat of April 30, were beginning to recover their good humor. General Vaillant's presence seemed to make them confident of victory. In short order, the sappers from the corps of engineers chopped down a small woodlot located close to the Casa Mattei, near the Via Portuense. They were laughing happily. Nothing gave them as much pleasure as these works of destruction. They were overjoyed when they demolished a house and delirious when they razed a palace to the ground.

Henri and Annibal were always together, whether the lieutenant was overseeing the work or whether they were walking around the outskirts of Rome. While the artillerymen were making their gabions from grape vines, the two friends often came into contact with the deafest unit in the French armies. They had long hours in which to chat, and the hours had to be long, for their poor eardrums, pierced by the frightful detonations of mortars or shattered by the explosion of artillery pieces loaded with grapeshot, were not at all amenable to spoken conversation. They had to bellow "good day" to them and roar "good evening." In that case, Annibal asked for a cannon as an interpreter.

Sometimes the two friends, accompanied by the valiant Jean Taupin, walked up to the walls of Rome, even chatting on many occasions with the Romans. Several times the Romans let French soldiers into the city, which they inspected in detail. It even happened that important persons, disguised as peasants, doctors, etc., went to check out the defensive fortifications for themselves.

Indeed, the Romans appeared to have no doubt that a peace would soon be signed. Proud of their first victory, they even seemed to consider themselves entitled to dictate its conditions. No longer attaching any importance to the presence of the French army under their walls, they allowed the foreigners to go in and out at will. Roman workers even carried out repairs every day on the church of San Paolo, about half a league down from Rome, on the left bank of the Tiber. They could be seen setting up, for the exterior decorations, the beautiful marble columns that had recently been given to Pope Pius IX.

Often the Romans even came to the French camp, but these visits created no difficulty, since preparations for the siege had not yet begun. One day the triumvirs were supposed to pay a visit to the commander-in-chief. In order to receive them in a more dignified manner, he had the army's gabions and fascines drawn up in two rows, since he had nothing

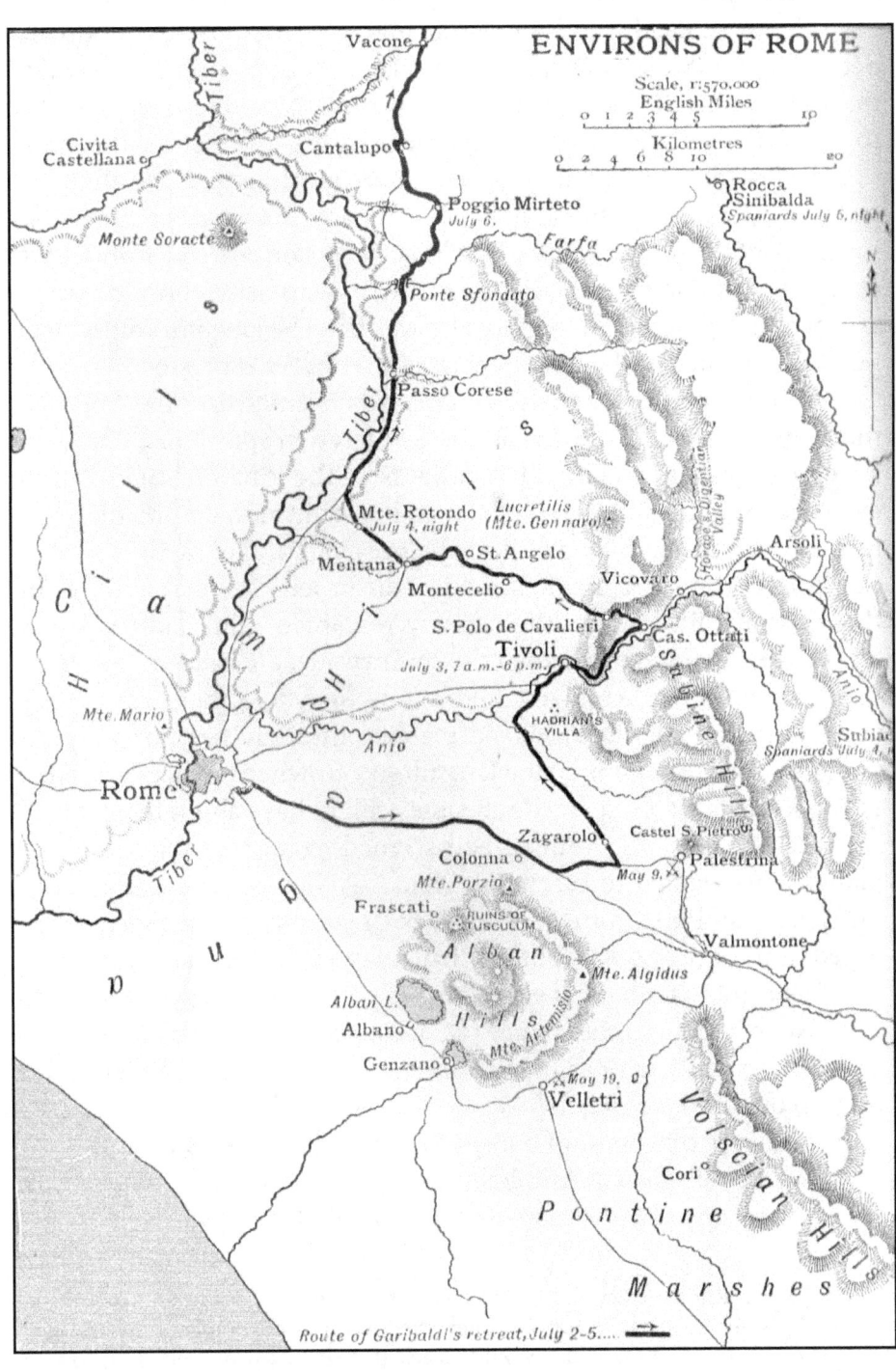

ENVIRONS OF ROME

Scale, 1:570,000
English Miles
0 1 2 3 4 5   10
Kilometres
0 2 4 6 8 10   20

Vacone

Civita
Castellana
Cantalupo

Poggio Mirteto
July 6.

Rocca
Sinibalda
Spaniards July 6, night

Monte Soracte

Farfa

Ponte Sfondato

Passo Corese

Mte. Rotondo
July 4, night

Lucretilis
(Mte. Gennaro)

Arsoli

Mentana
St. Angelo

Montecelio
Vicovaro

S. Polo de Cavalieri

Tivoli
July 3, 7 a.m.–6 p.m.
Cas. Ottati

Mte. Mario
HADRIAN'S
VILLA

Rome
Anio
Subia
Spaniards July 4,

Zagarolo
Castel S. Pietro

Colonna
Palestrina

Mte. Porzio
May 9,

Frascati
RUINS OF
TUSCULUM
Valmontone

Alban
Mte. Algidus

Alban L.

Albano
Hills
Mte. Artemisio

Genzano

May 19.
Velletri

Cori

Pontine

Volscian Hills

Marshes

Route of Garibaldi's retreat, July 2–5.

more triumphal available in the way of decoration. But this magnificent avenue of dead wood was not inaugurated, because the triumvirs decided not to leave Rome. A few days later, rumors of a royal visit ran through the headquarters. A Roman princess was said to be coming to honor the French army's encampment with her presence. The commander-in-chief could not have been more gracious and chivalrous to this noble person and the ladies of her company. But what was the astonishment of the rank-and-file foot-soldiers when, on entering Rome, they recognized, among the lower-class women of the city, those beautiful aristocratic ladies whose only royalty was their beauty and whose only nobility consisted of the sentiments that they never expressed .

At this juncture Garibaldi and his troops entered Rome. Soon, in the presence of the French army (a disinterested spectator), that bold adventurer began to harass the soldiers of the king of Naples. Soon even the king himself took flight with his army and, despite his artillery and war materiel, fled in haste before a handful of men.[7]

Apart from that incident, which disturbed the surroundings of the city for a little while, the country remained calm and secure. A few isolated marauders roamed the countryside, but caused no serious damage. Henri and Annibal could not possibly lose their way among the countless roads cutting at sharp angles through the vineyards and orchards, for the summit of the Janicululm, crowned by the dome of St. Peter's, always resolved any doubts they might have about their route.

For several days, Annibal had seemed to be resisting the secret plans Henri wanted to carry out. Henri scolded his friend for being unfriendly and his brother for his lack of courage. In the evening he urged him more strongly, but the lieutenant still refused.

"All right, Annibal, I'll go by myself."

"No, no, Henri, that's out of the question."

"I'll certainly have as much courage as most of our soldiers, who only go out of idle curiosity."

"But we're officers, and our uniforms will get us into trouble."

"We'll be disguised. Annibal, this is the last time I'm going to talk to you about my plan. Tomorrow, at daybreak, I'll go by myself."

---

7. This exploit is an example of Garibaldi's daring moves. Verne shows later on that they would be repeated and intensified to raise the morale of the besieged citizens. In 1860 Garibaldi would attack the Kingdom of Naples again and occupy it.

A Sapper in 1853.

"But really, who have you got a grudge against?" retorted the lieutenant, at his wits' end.

"If I knew that, I wouldn`t have a grudge against him any longer, because I'd already have my revenge."

"Look here, Henri, you've got some bold undertaking in mind. I can't change your mind about it, but I'll help you with all my courage. We'll go together."

"Tomorrow," went on the young captain eagerly. "The negotiations are coming to an end. The truce will soon be over and then it will be too late."

"Tomorrow," replied Annibal sadly, "we'll go into Rome."

The commander-in-chief had occupied the important positions around Rome. The fort of Salo, occupied by a few troops, maintained land communications with Civitavecchia and the little Mediterranean port of Fiumicino, at the mouth of the Tiber, which he had ordered the navy to protect.

The Tiber, Castle St. Angelo, and St. Peter's in Rome, 1903.

On the appointed day the two young men, disguised as peasants, appeared at the outposts, accompanied by Jean Taupin. The Romans let them in with no difficulty, and they climbed over the barricade erected in front of the Porta Portese. Following Via San Michelo and Via Santa Maria, they reached the middle of the Trastevere, a part of the city built on the Janiculum, on the right bank of the Tiber. This is the most unusual part of Rome, from the point of view of monuments, whereas the old city, on the left blank of the river, is more spacious and more archaeological, and rich in ruins and antiquities.

But Henri had not come to admire; he had come to see and reconnoiter. He stared at the Romans with an insulting persistence that might have got him into trouble. Annibal followed his friend without saying a word, and Taupin showed them the way. The three Frenchmen soon reached St. Peter's Square. Henri, gloomier than ever, scrutinized every passer-by. Only a madman would have hoped to meet someone in that big city, but no one has ever said that Henri was not mad. Otherwise he would already have died of despair. But his search proved fruitless. He walked quickly down towards the Tiber, passed the Castel Sant'Angelo, and went on towards the Corso. Just as he got to that lovely street, lined with palaces, where his companions rejoined him, he found himself in the midst of a large crowd. Probably one of the many Roman street orators was recounting a few of his bold exploits, with a great display of eloquence, quite unflattering to the French army. The young captain was about to keep on going and resume the course of his rash investigations, when a woman's screams brought him to a sudden stop. They were a kind of groan interspersed with meaningless words and vague ideas that were soon drowned out by the crowd's shouts of rage.

"It's the mad woman, the mad Frenchwoman," exclaimed the onlookers.

"What are they going on about?" asked Annibal. "Is it…?"

But the lieutenant's friend gripped his hand so tightly and furiously that he did not finish his sentence.

"Well, what is this?" he said.

"Let's get out of here," replied Jean Taupin. "Daggers are quickly drawn and used in this country."

"Henri, are you coming?" said Annibal.

Henri was no longer with them.

"Henri! Henri!" he shouted.

"This way, lieutenant, this way," shouted Jean Taupin.

The sapper, dragging Annibal out of the crowd, pointed to a frenzied girl who was running down the Corso at an incredible speed. Henri was following her, but losing ground, because he seemed to be growing weaker at every step. The poor woman was waving her arms around and running madly from side to side as she fled towards the Capitole.

"The madwoman! The mad Frenchwoman!" the foolish crowd kept howling.

"Beware of the Tarpeian rock," they were saying, without making a move to help the unfortunate woman.

And indeed there was reason to fear that she might hurl herself off that steep height.

"Help! Help me!" shouted Henri, trying vainly to catch up with her. "It's her! It's her! It's Marie!"

His two companions flew after him and soon caught up with him. But without slackening the lightning rapidity of her pace, the girl had run down the steps of the Capitole, or rather slid down them like a phantom. At every step she could have been killed. The crowd blocking the streets opened superstitiously to make way for her. Eventually she reached the ancient Forum and collapsed as if dead on the capital of a fallen column. But suddenly, standing up as if she were inspired, she cried out, "Woe, woe, woe to Rome! Woe to infamy, whatever clothes it may wear and by whatever name it may be called. Woe to those who have destroyed me, for I have been chosen by God to be the occasion for his wrath."

The people listened and trembled. Suddenly a man approached the mad woman.

"Get back, "he shouted. "This woman is mine."

The poor girl fainted when she saw him. It was Andreani.

Then Henri and his two friends arrived on the scene.

"It's him! At last! It's him!" shouted the unfortunate captain, and he fell to the ground, stabbed in the arm by a stiletto.

"Fall back!" cried Annibal. "Come here, Jean Taupin!"

The tall, powerful sapper picked up his friend and quickly ran away. When he was outside the city, Henri regained consciousness, but he was weakened by his wound and his emotions, and needed the help of several soldiers to get back to camp.

When the two officers reached San Carlo, Jean Taupin was no longer with them. The next day the truce expired.

Chapter III

THE SIEGE

THE FRENCH AMBASSADOR TO ROME had negotiated vigorously, but he had been outmaneuvered by the machinations of the triumvirs and had soon found himself, almost without realizing it, in too republican a mood for an overly rebellious power.[1] As a result, he brought to the council of generals a treaty that was anything but honorable for France. The Duke de Reggio, also confused by the convoluted diplomatic eloquence, was about to agree to the treaty, and even sign it, when the mysterious influence that had been his guardian angel took control of him, something that he would never have reason to regret.

And so the treaty was rejected and the truce came to an end. The order to attack came from Paris. Once the armistice had been revoked, the rumor was allowed to circulate through the camp that the attack would not begin until June 4. The Romans were taken in and caught by surprise, for the French columns began to move at 4 a.m. on June 3.

The troops defending Rome were quite different from the Roman troops. The triumvirs, Armellini, Mazzani, and Saffi, had chosen Garibaldi as their general. This Piedmontese adventurer possessed tremendous organizational talent. He created wonderful resources for himself in the midst of the most insurmountable difficulties, and had no trouble disciplining the most unruly of men. This republican Fra Diavolo, who always wore dramatic, bright-colored clothes, ruled by terror and prestige. His personal troops consisted of a regiment of

---

1. The French Ambassador was Ferdinand de Lesseps (1805-1894), who would later construct the Suez Canal, opened in 1869 by the Empress Eugénie, wife of Napoleon III.

lancers and a legion of infantry six thousand strong. Around him rallied the Lombards (whose young officers belonged to the leading families of Lombardy), the two regiments of the Union Romaine, the pope's dragoons and carabineers, the municipal guard (which was on duty in the interior of the city), and finally the Swiss artillerymen, the best marksmen in Europe, newly arrived from the siege of Bologna, where they had held the Austrians off for a long time. Rome was therefore valiantly defended. Its arsenals were filled with munitions and its walls bristled with a hundred and twenty cannon.

There was no thought of surrounding Rome, or of starving it into submission. The French army numbered only twenty thousand men at that time, not enough to surround a city with a circumference of eighteen kilometers, especially when it was fully supplied with food and ammunition. Once the idea of surrounding the city was rejected and the decision made to attack, the discussion centered on the point of attack and was elucidated by the splendid ideas of General Vaillant.

The new Rome includes all of the old one and extends over both banks. One of the highest mountains within it is the Janiculum, a seemingly impregnable hill. It is located on the right bank of the Tiber and dominates the entire city. It is protected by a fortified enclosure that runs from the river and the Porta Portese to Castel Sant'Angelo, and is also intersected by the old Aurelian wall, forming, behind the enclosure, a large interior retrenchment running from the Porta Portese to the Porta San Pancrazio. That side of Rome, protected by a double wall, is therefore much stronger than the other part of the city, which is surrounded only by the old enclosure, and it seemed more natural to attack through one of the points on the left bank. But despite the opinion of the artillery, General Vaillant explained that an attack from the right bank, although longer and more difficult, was nevertheless more logical and safer. Communication with the army remained open and, as soon as the Janiculum was occupied, the city would be taken. Dominated by the enemy, it could be crushed by their bombs, whereas, once the left wall was penetrated, the soldiers would have to wage a deadly and interminable war of barricades with the Romans. Finally, it was essential not to appear to be acting in conjunction with the Austrians and Neapolitans encamped to the east of the city. In France, it was claimed that the main reason for attacking through the Janiculum was to save the Roman monuments. The truth was that they did not concern themselves in the least with such delicate archaeological matters and attacked on the right bank because that was the way it had to be.

The general of artillery deferred to General Vaillant's opinion. In the event of a disagreement, the commander-in-chief would have had the final word. Consideration had also been given to capturing Castel Sant'Angelo. That was the opinion of Louis-Napoléon Bonaparte, the president of the French Republic, who must have been very well informed, since he had lived in Rome for a long time. [2] According to him, the Romans would not admit defeat until that fortress had been occupied. However, this proposal was rejected and the Janiculum was chosen as the point of attack.

It is a general principle of military engineering to attack through a salient rather than through an indentation. A breach is made in a bastion rather than through the curtain between two bastions, since they protect each other and their cross-fire makes it impossible to approach

2.   Louis-Napoléon Bonaparte (1808-1873) was the nephew of Napoleon I, and inherited the leadership of the Bonapartist movement with the return of the monarchy. When it was deposed with the revolution of February 1848, and the Second Republic was established in France, he was elected President on December 10, 1848 with 75% of the votes cast. Forbidden under the constitution to seek re-election, he seized dictatorial powers on December 2, 1851, the 47th anniversary of Napoleon I's crowning as Emperor, before his own ascension as Emperor Napoleon III a year later. Victor Hugo went into exile after the coup, labeling him as "Napoléon le Petit" ("Napoleon the Small"), a mere mediocrity.

Under the rule of Napoleon III, the French economy was rapidly modernized, with industrialization, the expansion of railroads, the construction of the Suez Canal, and the rebuilding of Paris. He sought to reassert French influence in Europe and abroad, and in this way is perhaps best remembered in the United States for attempting to place Maximillian I on the throne of Mexico during the American Civil War. Napoleon III fell from power when Otto von Bismarck manipulated him into beginning the disastrous Franco-Prussian War, and after several months he was captured at the Battle of Sedan and deposed by the Third Republic two days later, on September 4, 1870.

Having lived in Italy as a young man, Napoleon III had associated with the revolutionaries. However, to court Catholic support he sent French troops to help restore Pope Pius IX as ruler of the Papal States, although he tried to please all sides by demanding that the pope introduce liberal changes and sent an emissary to negotiate with the Italian nationalist Mazzini. Napoleon supported the ideal of Italian nationalism, a favorite cause of the left in France, and toward this end went to war with Austria in 1859, but withdrew in time for most of the Papal states to be incorporated into the new Italian state, with only French troops keeping Rome from seizure by the Italian government. The seemingly vacillating policy satisfied no one.

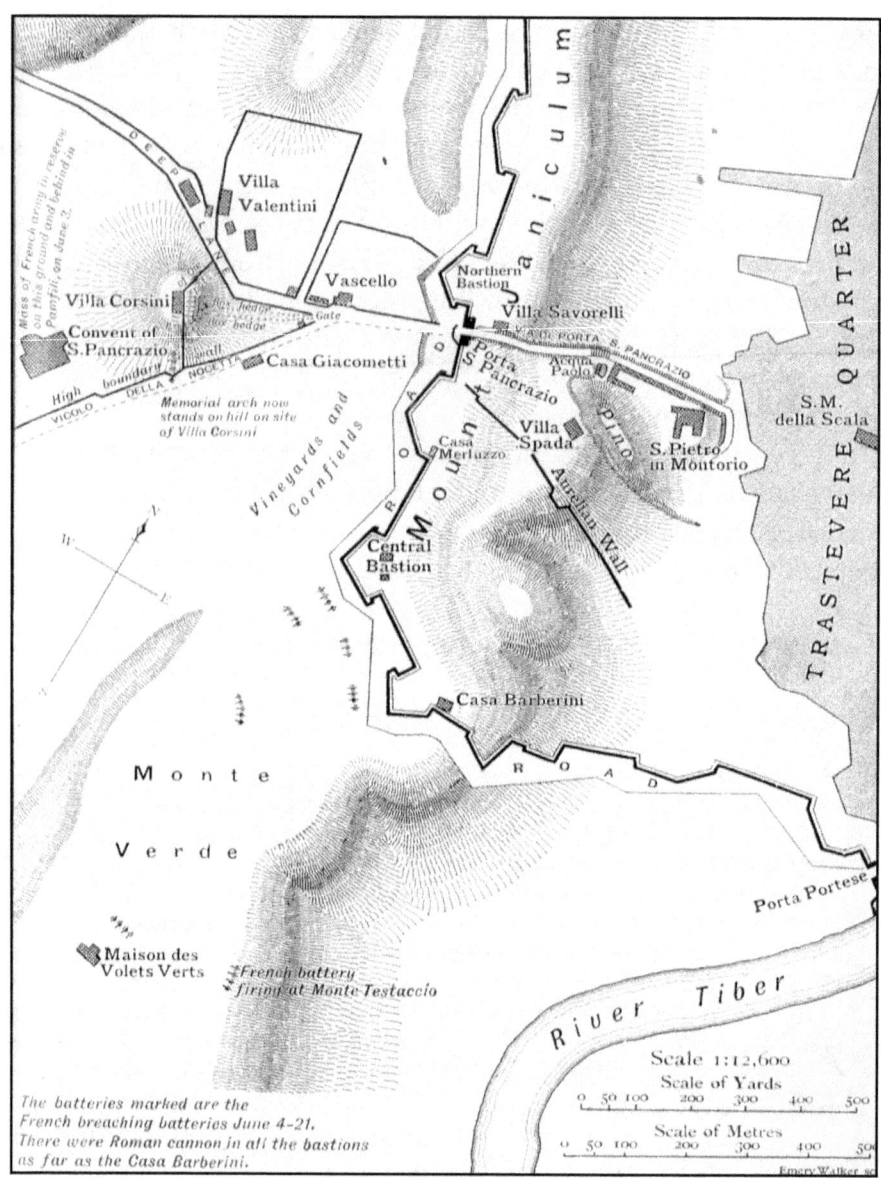

Battle of Villa Corsini, June 3, and first part of siege, June 4 – 21.

the curtain.[3] The attack must also be made as far as possible from two gates through which the enemy might make a sortie. What was the position, then?

The point of the Janiculum is a salient, flanked by two bastions and protected by a demilune, a sort of semi-circular retrenchment in

---

3.   A curtain is the part of a defensive wall joining two bastions.

front of the curtain, and dominated by it. Despite its strength, this salient was chosen as the point of attack. It is located half-way between the Porta Portese and the Porta San Pancrazio, which are separated from each other by seven bastions.

The Romans, however, had not been idle during the truce. Huge barricades had been set up in the city, and all the streets leading to it had been cut by trenches and blocked by excavations lined with steps and banquettes for the fusiliers. On General Vaillant's orders, a colonel, a captain, and a number of sappers carried out a reconnaissance as far as the walls of Rome. They found the Porta San Pancrazio and the adjoining ramparts padded and lined with bags of earth. Battlements had been put up on the walls, using little fruit-vendor's baskets, which the Romans had begun collecting by the thousands. Formidable batteries were erected on Monte Testaccio and Monte Sant'Aventino, near the church of Sant'Alessis. This church is located on the left bank of the Tiber, opposite the Porta Portese, which opens onto the right bank. The Testaccio is a little hummock about a hundred and twenty feet high, formed by a large heap of old pottery, five hundred meters to the south of Monte Sant'Aventino. The territory occupied by the French army sloped down to the river and these various batteries would be able to destroy it without hindrance.

Little by little, the Romans armed four bastions. The first flanked the right side of the Porta San Pancrazio as you leave the city, and there were three others in a row to the left. The last two were located precisely at the Janiculum salient, and the first attacks were to be directed against them. The space between the fortified enclosure and the old Aurelian wall was cut by trenches and strewn with defense works. In front of the church of San Pietro in Montorio, new batteries were set up on the old wall, and from there the Romans could destroy their own bastions if they should be taken by storm. To the left of these batteries, not more than a hundred meters from the Porta San Pancrazio, stood the house that Garibaldi had taken for his headquarters.

The line of attack had to be maintained, and in order to do that, both ends of it had to be occupied. It was necessary, therefore, to capture the plateau facing the part of the Janiculum that was to be besieged. On the extreme left of that plateau stood the magnificent villas of Pamphili, Valentini, and Corsini, and the church of San Pancrazio. On the far right stood Monte Verde. The line of attack, thirteen hundred meters long, was to advance between those two points, the Corsini plateau and Monte Verde. The troops from Mattei were encamped to the north of the Corsini plateau, and those from Santucci, the headquarters, to the south of Monte Verde. The operations of the siege, perfectly regular and precise, were thus concentrated on the salient points of the Janiculum, between the road to Civitavecchia and the Via Portuense. Monte Verde was not more than eight hundred meters from San Carlo, where the engineers were billeted.

It was on this rugged terrain, crossed by several roads, covered with country houses, and dotted with high vineyards and orchards, that the magnificent siege operations were to be carried out, led by General Vaillant. The attack began by taking the outposts.

At three o'clock on the morning of June 3, General Jean Levaillant's brigade, led by Major Frossard of the engineers, advanced to occupy the plateau on which the three villas, Corsini, Valentini, and Pamphili, were located. In the latter, the Romans, who were drinking, were caught off guard by the arrival of the French. With a bag of gunpowder, the sappers opened a breach in the outer wall. The effect of these explosions is tremendous. An eight-kilogram bag of gunpowder, covered with a stone, a plank, or some other object, in order to concentrate its effect, is sufficient to destroy an oak door ten centimeters thick. The French slipped through the opening and overwhelmed the Romans at bayonet-point. But the explosion had set off the alarm, the defense was organized, and the Lombard volunteers withdrew into the villas of Corsini and Valentini. The French brigade charged forward and occupied two new points fairly close to the square, but the batteries at the Porta San Pancrazio soon overwhelmed them with cannonballs and shells. The French were forced to evacuate the villas and the Lombards boldly reoccupied them. These positions changed hands four times. General Regnault Saint-Jean-d'Angély fought like a rank-and-file soldier. When he saw a company hesitating, he took command of it and led it into battle. Finally, at five o'clock, the Villa Corsini, enveloped in flames, remained in the hands of the French, who took up a solid position in order not to be disturbed by the cannon from the square. The point of departure for the operations on the left flank, the Corsini plateau, was now occupied.

Meanwhile, it was decided to capture Monte Verde, which would serve as the point of departure for operations on the right flank. Anni-

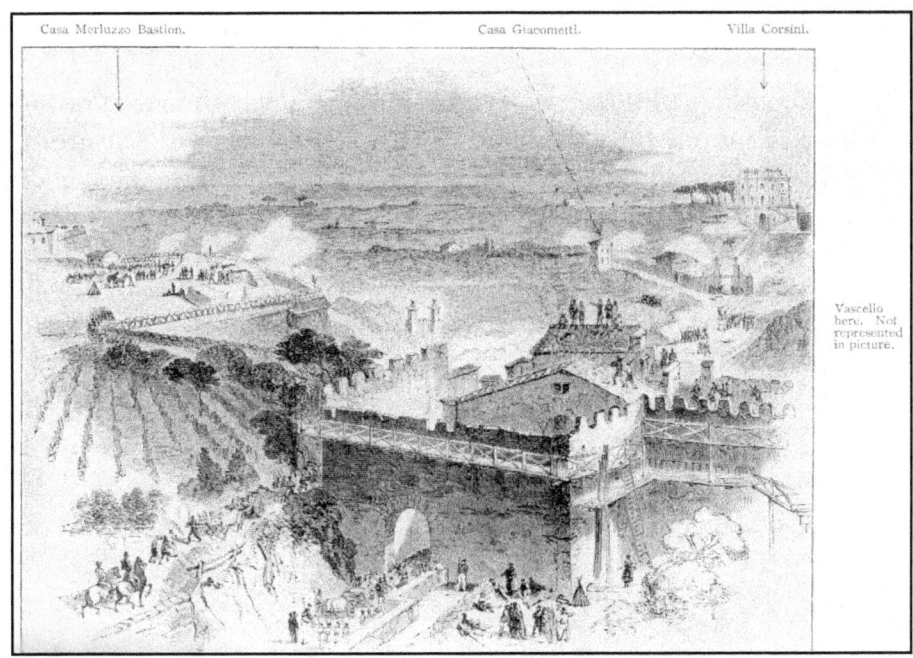

Casa Merluzzo Bastion.   Casa Giacometti.   Villa Corsini.

Vascello here. Not represented in picture.

Porto San Pancrazio from inside on June 3, 1849, from *Illustrated London News.*

bal's company, part of the first regiment of engineers, left San Carlo at three o'clock in the morning under the command of Captain de Jous-lard, and reached a house seven hundred meters forward of the camp and six hundred meters from the square. This house had a ground floor with stone steps leading up to it and an upper story with six windows facing Rome. They called it the green-shuttered house. The French went there to take cover. Annibal was ordered to occupy a little cabin on the right, which overlooked the valley of the Tiber and offered a view of part of Rome. After stationing his sentinels, he made himself at home in the house, and he and the second lieutenant went upstairs to lie down on the straw. Suddenly a cannonball came through the room and covered them with debris.

"Are you wounded?" asked Annibal.

"No," replied his comrade.

"Let's get going, then!"

They hurried downstairs and took cover with the soldiers behind the house. The batteries on Monte Aventino and Testacccio were thundering without letup, and debris was falling on Annibal's men. Instead of looking up to avoid it, they hunched their backs and simply let it fall on their heads. The lieutenant called them ostriches, but when he saw that the position was no longer tenable, he abandoned the cabin, leaving one sentinel there, and fell back to the green-shuttered house. All the buildings behind the line connecting the villas with the green-shuttered house fell into the hands of the attackers. The occupation of the Corsini plateau and Monte Verde formed the line of attack that would envelop the point of the Janiculum.

In order to deceive the besieged troops and prevent them as long as possible from knowing what point was threatened, the commander-in-chief deployed the troops encamped at Ponte-Molle on the opposite side of the city. However, the Romans constructed a battery at the angle of the bastion closest to Monte Verde, and opened fire on the green-shuttered house on the morning of June 4. Captain de Jouslard, who was occupying it, ordered the soldiers to take cover behind the

Louis-Napoléon Bonaparte.

walls. As Annibal was coming down the front steps, a naval officer, who was following the campaign as an observer, was struck in the chest by a cannonball, which then decapitated one soldier and shattered the hand of another. When the Romans no longer saw anyone, they held their fire, thinking the house had been evacuated.

These isolated battles, made necessary by the siege of the Janiculum, were very bloody. Two hundred and eighty men and fourteen officers were killed or wounded. Many of those unfortunate men called for a priest as they fell, but they died without consolation and without prayers. The war budget, which amounted to nearly three hundred and fifty million, could not afford to pay a chaplain.

The deadliest actions, comparatively speaking, were over. Rome would be taken, precisely as planned, and without a great deal of bloodshed. A small house in front of San Carlo became the trench storeroom. A dressing station was set up there, as well as at the Villa Pamphili and the church of San Pancrazio. There were two other dressing stations, one at Monte Mario and another at Santucci, the headquarters.

The trenches were about to be opened at last.

To reach the enclosure of a besieged city without danger a trench is dug, six or seven feet deep, parallel to the walls, and the earth is thrown up on the side towards the enemy. This trench must be wide enough to allow gun-carriages to pass through, so that batteries can be set up at the necessary points. When the first parallel trench has been dug in this way, usually about a thousand meters from the square, branch lines are dug leading toward the city, taking cover from the dangerous spots. Then a second parallel trench is dug, and a third, closing in more and more on the point of attack. It is clear, therefore, that the batteries, each one closer than the last, can now begin breaking down the walls. To take cover from a dangerous spot involves digging a trench in such a way that projectiles coming from that spot do not travel through its entire length. In short, it means laying it out almost at right angles to the lines of fire. That explains the many zigzags in the trenches and branch lines, which turn this way and that, move forward and back as they progress, and by their carefully planned changes of direction confront all the dangerous points.

For working in the trench, the engineering troops were divided into three brigades, each under the command of an officer. There were in all twelve hundred workmen and fifteen hundred guards. General

Rostolan, with the rest of the troops, took up a position at the center of the operations to support the endangered points.

The first parallel trench, which ran from the church of San Pancrazio to the little house briefly occupied by Annibal, was thirteen hundred meters long. It was divided into two attacking forces. The one on the left was assigned to Major Galbaud Dufort and Captain Boissonet. The one on the right would be led by Major Goury and Captain de Jouslard.

On the night of June 4 to 5, as soon as it was dark enough to conceal the city and the camp, the workers, carrying shovels and picks, and with their rifles slung on their backs, moved silently to the green-shuttered house and were stationed along the length of the parallel trench, whose route had been previously mapped out at the headquarters of the engineering corps. When the signal was given, every worker set about digging a hole in the ground, into which he crouched. Then he deepened, widened, and lengthened it, in the most orderly fashion and in complete safety. Meanwhile, the troops from Ponte-Molle created a diversion by making a feint at the Porta del Popolo. It was a bold plan and a dangerous undertaking to trace out this trench so close to the square, for at some points it was no more than two hundred meters away. But General Vaillant was astute enough to know what kind of enemies he was dealing with. His caution was both daring and cunning.

The artillery began setting up its batteries immediately. The first one, placed in front of the green-shuttered house, was to fire back at the battery in the bastion to the right of the Janiculum salient. The second was installed at the far right of the trench, in order to reply vigorously to the batteries at Testaccio and Monte Aventino. Both were protected by a parapet fitted with embrasures. The first battery, armed with two sixteen-pounders and a field howitzer, and the second, with two twenty-four-pounders and a field howitzer, opened a very heavy fire on the morning of June 5.

Trenches were dug at night and widened during the day. Although the Romans kept up a sustained fire, the soldiers easily became accustomed to it, thumbing their noses at the cannonballs passing over their heads. They had few dangers to contend with. But the besieged troops soon noticed that the infantry were relieved every morning and afternoon at four o'clock, and directed their fire at the brigades approaching or leaving the trenches. To offset this danger, a covered road was built

Monte Testaccio.

during the night of June 5 to 6 behind the trench and connecting it to the trench storeroom, so that the soldiers could get to work without any danger.

Henri, confined to the dressing station at San Carlo, was still suffering from his wound. His blood, heated by emotion and despair, irritated the wound and prevented it from healing. Annibal went to see him whenever he was off duty. Henri was sure the valiant Jean Taupin had fallen victim to his devotion to duty, and his continuous feverish dreams about the poor mad woman also spoke to him about the unfortunate soldier.

"He went there to die," said Henri.

"No," replied the lieutenant, "he stayed there to avenge you."

But the young captain's heart could not regain its confidence, as he writhed in pain on his bed.

The work of widening the trench continued without letup. The Roman batteries now had vigorous adversaries, who kept them occupied and fired back at them constantly. The artillery was in charge of choosing an emplacement for batteries, which would begin breaking through the walls. They built a third one near the middle of the trench, about two hundred and twenty meters from the square. It was made up of mortars capable of lobbing shells into the bastions, and was armed during the night of June 7 to 8. At the same time, a line was dug from the trench, leading to the right, by making a little detour, in such a way as to be protected from Testaccio and Monte Aventino. Connecting lines, which would lead to the gun emplacement in the second trench, wound their way towards the square. The operations were often interrupted by storms, but the work had been well done and was proof against landslides.

Piazza San Pietro, 1835.

To put a stop to the Roman bombardment, when it was too strong during the day, infantrymen from Vivienne hid in the church of San Pancrazio, the Villa Corsini, and the trenches. From a distance of six hundred meters and more, these splendid snipers killed the Roman artillerymen, firing through the embrasures. Their rifles, crafted with rare perfection and equipped with a graduated sight that instantly calculated the distance by which a bullet would drop at any given range, enabled them to hit their targets accurately at incredible distances. These skilled soldiers were soon overwhelmed by the wreckage of the Villa Corsini, and a trench was dug farther back, where they would be protected from the cannon on the wall while they fired.

About eight o'clock on the evening of June 9, the besieged troops attempted to make a sortie through the Porta San Pancrazio. An unusual sort of barricade, made of barrels, which they rolled in front of them, enabled them to take up a position in the vineyards. They set up a deadly fusillade from there, but a frightful thunderstorm soon forced them to retreat back into the city.

The work went on during the following nights. Sometimes the route was not followed exactly, and the trenches came under direct fire, either from the batteries at the Vatican or from those on the ramparts. But the valiant soldiers were not discouraged. They were able to correct the error the following night, and the city, without knowing it, was being hemmed in more and more closely. Almost all the work was done "on the fly." The workers simply pushed a few gabions ahead of them and filled them with earth. Behind this light shelter they dug a hole, crouched down in it and enlarged it. Working behind a moving protective shield and wearing a helmet slowed the operation down too much for their liking.

During the night of June 10 to 11, the workers struck a wall. It was the wall of a demilune. As General Vaillant had foreseen, it protected the curtain between the two bastions against which the attack was concentrated.

The artillery, for its part, had not been idle. During the night of June 8 to 9, it had installed a fourth battery near the mortars, a hundred and seventy-five meters from the square, to open a breach in the right-hand bastion. During the night of June 10 to 11, a fifth battery was set up, a hundred and twenty-five meters away, to attack the right flank of the left-hand bastion. Finally, to the right of the Villa Corsini, a

Villa Corsini, the facade after the Italian cannonade.

sixth battery would attack the left flank of the same bastion. The installation of three demolition batteries was decided on, but they were not yet armed, for the roads were impassable. And so the siege operations were carried out precisely, and could lead to only one definite result.

Around one o'clock in the morning, the besieged troops launched a huge fire ship against the Passera Bridge, but it was spotted in time and a few volleys of cannon fire soon sank it.

The second trench was now nearly finished. Starting from the salient on the demilune, it ran alongside the small wall on the left. The work went on quietly. There was no indication of an imminent attack by the Romans, and the only significant event of the night was the capture of eighty wagons full of ammunition, food, and wine, which were taken by General Morris at the head of his cavalry and a battalion of infantry. But at eight o'clock in the morning, four companies from the Union Regiment, which had advanced under cover by the wall of the demilune, leaped into a section of the trench, occupying it momentarily and exchanging fire with the men of the 55th infantry. Henri Formont, whose wound no longer kept him confined to camp, was excited by the nearby explosions and hurried to the scene of battle.

He fought heroically, madly, desperately, beside Colonel Niel of the engineers, who was directing the defense. He wielded his sword without letup for three-quarters of an hour. Finally the Romans withdrew back into the city, leaving about forty of their men behind. The workmen laid down their powder-blackened muskets and returned to the task of widening the trench.

During the night of June 12 to 13, the second trench, now completely finished, was opened to the artillery teams. As the general had promised, the three demolition batteries and the mortar battery were ready to open fire.

Chapter IV

THE ATTACKS

THE BOLD LEADERS WHO GOVERNED the republic urged the people to defend the city, but the peaceable citizens, pressed into service within the city, had lost their enthusiasm for going up to the walls. The municipal guard, unaccustomed to a hail of bullets and staggered by the skill of the Orleans infantry, were a sorry sight as they made their way to the ramparts. Since these unfortunate second-hand soldiers were not relieved until they had used up all their ammunition, they hurriedly fired in all directions and ran away when they had not a single cartridge left on their consciences.

The triumvirs, however, tried in every possible way to restore public morale. They spread news of great triumphs. The defeat of April 30 was proclaimed as a tremendous victory. It was the important word on the agenda. The flight of the King of Naples before Garibaldi's legion was described in various and most glowing terms, and its date took on historic importance.

The slow pace of the siege made the besieged troops laugh. They did not suspect that their defeat was inevitable. The French were not trying to enter sooner or later, but simply to enter. General Vaillant, in his genius and solicitude, made every effort to respect the lives of his soldiers, while also doing his duty. His losses were therefore only minor. If the Roman garrison had known more about siege warfare, they would have at least threatened some of the besiegers' operations, or even stopped them. They would have understood that their surrender was the inevitable result of a geometrical problem.

Andreani was actively involved in all this rabble-rousing by the triumvirs. The woman he had taken away from Henri's pursuit had not reappeared on the streets of Rome, but she did not occupy his time to such an extent that he could not participate actively in the defense and do his utmost everywhere. In that scene of madness and blood, he had recognized the French officer and was aware of the connection between him and the young woman. But the traitor did not know he was being followed, spied on, and driven by the valiant Jean Taupin. As soon as he saw the young captain fall, that bold soldier had set out on Andreani's trail. After following the ex-secretary along a thousand detours and collecting useful details about him, he had thought about returning to his camp, but the gates of Rome were shut, and the next day the truce was permanently ended.

Jean Taupin was now a prisoner, although he had not been recognized, and his prison was the entire city. He made up his mind to solve the mystery that had led him into that perilous situation. Since there must have been some secret feeling connecting Henri Formont to that unfortunate mad woman, he had to find out what power Andreani held over the girl, what his intentions were, and in what shameful labyrinth of infamy and servitude she was imprisoned.

Every evening, at nightfall, Andreani went out by the Porta San Pancrazio. Jean Taupin did not know where he was going and, being reluctant to undergo close scrutiny by the sentinels, he did not dare venture outside the city. But Andreani could not go far, for he would soon have encountered the French advance posts. Taupin confined himself to making observations inside the city, but he found nothing that could put him on the trail of that infamous deed.

Andreani had taken on the role of town crier of misinformation. He actively peddled news of false victories, which the masses imagined they had won over the besiegers. He had often frightened the triumvirs by his fits of anger, just as Hébert used to terrify the moderates of the Convention, Danton and Robespierre. The fact was that Andreani hated the French as an assassin hates his victim. He would have no compromise with his enemies, believing that they had all come there to avenge an insult to one person.

He went into a terrible rage, therefore, at six o'clock on the evening of June 12, when Major Poulle, on behalf of the commander-in-chief, brought the triumvirs the conditions of surrender. He personally tore up this proclamation, which was brought to the attention of the Roman citizenry:

> *"Citizens of Rome, we have been sent by the French Republic to carry out a conciliatory mission among you, but we have been received as enemies. Until now we have replied only mildly to the gunfire from your ramparts, but the time is approaching when the necessities of war will break out in terrible calamities. Do not let this horror befall a city filled with such glorious memories. Romans, accept us as mediators in your internal conflicts and do not take on yourselves the responsibility for irreparable disasters!"*

Since these conditions were not acceptable to enemies of tranquility and honor, the major returned to camp empty-handed. At six o'clock the next morning the order came from headquarters to open fire.

At that signal, the three demolition batteries fired in unison and the mortars showered missiles on the ramparts, making it extremely dangerous to stay there. A few of them even strayed as far as the Trastevere, spreading destruction and death when they exploded.

"Murderers!" shouted the Romans from the top of the walls. "Murderers, you are killing women and children!"

Disorder set in among their ranks. They fell back at first in the face of such deadly fire, but returned boldly to their posts. They aimed the many defense cannons in every direction, to such effect that by firing through the embrasures they again caught the French broadside and shot them down. They used whatever they could find to crush the besiegers: shovels, tongs, iron bars, stones, projectiles of every sort. Their cannons spat out death in a thousand forms. They even took advantage of the poor condition of the French missiles, for it is customary, during a campaign, to bring out the old ammunition from the magazines, leaving the new stock for little wars and parades. The shells often fell unexploded among the Romans, who loaded them into howitzers of the same caliber and sent them back, often with greater success.

Despite their efforts, the battery on the right-hand bastion was put out of action.

However, the demolition batteries positioned on the first trench found it difficult to make a hole in the bricks, which were held together by extremely hard cement. This was not because the batteries were too far from the square, but because the slope of the terrain prevented them from hitting the wall at the right spot. The way to open a breach is to fire at about two thirds of the wall, on two parallel horizontal lines, so that the space between those lines is pierced by cannonballs. This causes the wall to fall back on itself, filling in the trench and making it possible to get across it.

On the night of June 15 to 16, after new trenches tightened the grip on the city, the artillery began to build a seventh battery, located fifty meters from the square, to shell the curtain, and an eighth, forty-five meters away, to continue breaking down the right-hand bastion. They were both armed with guns from the first demolition batteries.

But now the gunfire from Testaccio broke out again with renewed violence, sweeping the trenches. Although the French were protected from head-on attacks, they had nothing to shield them from ricochets, and the shells that exploded in the trenches made them unusable. Then the commander-in-chief boldly and openly moved up a field piece to a protected position to the left of San Carlo. Its fire was surprisingly precise and daring. In one hour the battery on Testaccio was destroyed, and the mountain was littered with corpses.

New siege batteries were built the following night. The ninth was to attack the bastion on the left, while the tenth, situated near the Villa Corsini and much farther back than the others, was directed against the bastion to the left of the Porta San Pancrazio. Its orders were to fire back at the surrounding batteries, the houses of the bastions, the magnificent palace of Vascello, which stands to the left of the highway, and Garibaldi's house.

During the following night, work went ahead in front of the batteries, and a side trench was opened opposite each of the three breaches. On June 19, the new batteries opened fire. The Romans replied vigorously and the Testaccio batteries, which had been rebuilt during the night, became more troublesome than ever. An attempt to return fire with a field piece failed, and the second battery, on the extreme right of the trench, had to be rearmed in order to put them out of action.

For some time now, the Romans had been bringing into action the artillery at Castel Sant'Angelo, on the other side of the Janiculum, in an attempt to thwart the occupation of Ponte-Molle, but the French cannons answered back and soon destroyed the area extending from the Piazza del Popolo to Ponte-Molle.

During the next few nights the work of trenching continued. New trenches tightened the grip on the two bastions of the Porta San Pancrazio and formed a third parallel. The besiegers had now approached as close as possible to the bastions and to the curtain of the salient.

On June 21 the cannons kept up an all-day barrage. It could be seen that the breaches were now big enough to go through, and the attack was scheduled for the following night.

At eleven o'clock that evening, three columns, each made up of two companies of grenadiers and light infantry, were ordered to attack. Each one was led by an officer of the engineers, commanding a brigade of thirty sappers, whose function was to enlarge the breach. Half of the brigade marched behind the grenadiers, while the other half, carrying tools and bags of gunpowder, followed the light infantry. Major Galbaud Dufort led the attack.

Each column was to charge at one of the three breaches that had been opened in the two bastions and the curtain. The walls had been effectively knocked down by cannonballs, and each of the three connecting trenches, leading to the next parallel trench, ended in front of one of the breaches, thus enabling the attackers to remain under cover until they reached the wall.

Annibal and Henri were under the orders of Captain de Jouslard, who was leading the first column. It made a risky attack on the right-hand bastion. A house on top of the bastion had not been entirely destroyed and was full of defenders. A terrible fusillade burst forth from the two rows of windows.

"Fire!" shouted the valiant Captain de Jouslard.

Followed by Captain d'Astelet, he rushed towards the courtyard in front of the house, in order to break down the doors. His soldiers followed him. But as the two brave men were climbing over a low wall, they fell, mortally wounded.

"Forward!" shouted Annibal.

The sappers arrived, picked up Captain de Jouslard, and carried him to the green-shuttered house, where he died a few hours later.

"Blood and vengeance!" shouted Henri. The angry attackers, drunk with rage, quickly followed him. He reached the house, whose door was shattered by blows from rifle-butts and axes. The Romans tried in vain to stop the French from pouring in and to force them out of the ground floor, but they were crushed and torn apart by a moving wall of bayonets, which drove them back into a corner.

"Have mercy!" they pleaded as they knelt. "Have mercy!"

"No quarter!" cried Henri in a doleful voice, as his sabre was stained again and again with the blood of the vanquished. Not one of them survived that deadly combat,

However, the reserve workers had now arrived with their gabions, and the bastion was captured. The house was connected to the corner formed by the curtain and the bastion, so that it was closed at its narrowest point, and a trench came up to the breach behind.

The column attacking the curtain, which was only supposed to climb through the breach and stand ready to support one bastion or another, also lost a captain, and withdrew to the foot of the wall.

The Romans, in their ignorance, were not adequately prepared to repel the enemy. A few tarred fascines had been placed at the entrance to the breaches, but not properly ignited. They had also dug a few blast holes, which they did not detonate, and which were deactivated the next day. And yet, that was the surest way of slowing down the advance of the besiegers. Nothing is more terrifying to soldiers than the fear of these explosions. It does not take long to lay a mine. Six or seven sappers can easily dig a hole in one night, and by means of electricity and Bunsen batteries these deadly devices can go off at the desired moment. Ninety-three kilos of gunpowder, buried at a depth of four meters, will produce a crater with a radius of four meters. If several layers of mines are laid, enough earth can be moved to engulf entire companies. Nothing is more dreadful than gunpowder wounds. A bullet knocks a man to the ground and he lies there, motionless and speechless, but burns produce frightful screams and contortions of the damned. During the attack on Constantine, when a powder magazine exploded near the breach, the front ranks of soldiers were burned to a crisp, and the army watched as the other black soldiers, half burned, fled, filling the air with frightful howls.[1] Similarly, at the siege of Rome, the soldiers would have charged into the breaches with less enthusiasm if such an explosion had gone off under their feet.

---

1.   The city of Constantine was taken by Lamorcière on October 18, 1837.

But the Romans would still continue to defend themselves bravely. At daybreak new batteries were constructed in front of the church of San Pietro in Montorio and set up on the old Aurelian wall. Others were installed in the bastion to the right of the Porta San Pancrazio. The defense had now taken a big step backward. These batteries thundered out against the buildings captured during the night. Testaccio, repaired again and still formidable, opened fire once more. At seven in the morning the French were forced to abandon the house in the first bastion, which was falling in on them in ruins. The Romans occupied it again and barricaded themselves in it. An elite company charged boldly up to recapture it. Henri, not caring whether anyone was following him or not, ran around the bastion and, despite the fire from the batteries, despite the trenches furrowing the terrain, rushed towards the streets of Trastevere. Bullets were falling all around him. Cannonballs were digging up the earth and covering it with debris. He ran without stopping. Several Roman soldiers dashed after him. With his sabre, he tried to fend off the blows aimed at him. He was one man against twenty. He was about to perish when a strong arm came to his rescue.

"Hold on, captain," said a voice near him.

A few Frenchmen came to his assistance and the Romans were slowly pushed back. They abandoned the bastion for the second time, leaving about twenty dead behind. Henri was saved. He set out fiercely after the fleeing men.

"Not so fast, captain, and not so far."

Henri turned around to see Jean Taupin standing in front of him.

"Fall back," he said.

They both returned to the bastion where new retrenchments kept them safe from a *coup de main*.

Jean Taupin fell into Annibal and Henri's arms.

"I'll tell you my story soon," he said.

The French made use of the day to strengthen their position by deepening the trenches in such a way as to be protected from the danger spots. Two bastions had now been taken, and on their platforms French batteries would be erected to fire back at the new Roman fortifications. Four officers and thirty men had died during that glorious attack. The engineers, being the most exposed, had suffered the most. But General Vaillant had one foot in the door. He would not take long to put the other one in after it.

The next night, the two officers and Jean Taupin were together.

"You aren't dead!" Annibal said to him.

"Excuse me, lieutenant, I did everything necessary..."

"Necessary for that?"

"On the contrary, to live, and I succeeded fairly well."

"Jean," said Henri sadly.

"I'm sorry captain, excuse me. We should be speaking only for you. I didn't see that young woman again."

"Not once?"

"Not even once."

"Were you taken prisoner voluntarily?" asked the lieutenant.

"Very involuntarily. After the attack by that Italian, I chased after him. When I wanted to leave the city, the gates were closed and the truce had expired. After that, I made use of my forced imprisonment to shadow the assassin. I could have killed him, but..."

"You did well to let him live," said Henri coldly.

"That woman can't have left Rome," said Annibal.

"I don't think so, lieutenant, but I didn't see her again. I asked a number of people about the beautiful Frenchwoman, and I was told that she had come to Rome only three months ago. She was already out of her mind, and was apparently entrusted to the care of that Andreani."

"You know his name?" asked Henri, shuddering.

"Yes, and I know his profession too."

"A sort of aide-de-camp to Garibaldi?"

"Yes, he is now, but before the war he was the pope's private secretary."

"He's a priest!" exclaimed the young captain.

"No, he's a layman, which is no better. The pope dismissed him; no one knows why."

"I know! I know!" said Henri. "The pope must have known about his evil deeds. Oh, my poor Marie!"

"Henri," said Annibal, gripping his hand, "the time has come for you to confide in us. You can be sure that we're devoted to you, both this brave man who risked his life for you, and I myself, who would give my life for you. You may be killed in this campaign. Make a will as your heart dictates. Appoint one of us as the protector of the one you love, and the other as her avenger."

Henri seized their hands impulsively and said in a low voice, "Three months ago Marie and I were about to be married. I loved her then and I love her now. She was still not well. A terrible fright had nearly killed her. The victim of an attempted kidnapping, she was surrounded by invisible scoundrels who had designs on her honor. It was important that she should become my wife without delay, so that I would have the right to watch over her day and night. At last we were at the altar, and she had pledged before God her undying love for me. When the ceremony was over, as we were making our way through the crowd, a sudden, premeditated explosion spread confusion among those present. Thick smoke enveloped us. I hurried towards Marie, but – O my God! – she had disappeared. I had not seen her kidnapper, nor did I know his name. I was out of my mind for two days; otherwise I would have found her. As soon as I had partially regained my senses, I searched, I snooped, I spied. I learned that on our wedding day a postchaise had left town. I tracked it from one post house to another until I got to Marseille, where I heard that a man and a sick woman, who was supposed to be his sister, had embarked for Rome. God told me that it was Marie, and I was about to cross the sea myself, when war was declared. I obtained permission to fight on my own behalf, and here I am, before the insurmountable walls that hold the poor child. Oh! I'm madly in love. She has lost her mind. You saw her, just as I did. She didn't even recognize me. Sometimes I feel that her madness is affecting me, and I keep repeating, as she does, 'Woe is me! Woe is me!'"

The poor young man fell into a fit, which lasted until his comrades could bring him out of it.

"We'll avenge him," said Annibal to Taupin.

"Yes, lieutenant, but Fate has had a hand in all this. I'm familiar with such matters, and he is too unhappy ever to be happy again."

The three Frenchmen returned to their respective posts.

The two bastions of the salient had been taken, and the attack was now to be concentrated on the left. To take control of the Janiculum, they still had to capture the two bastions flanking the Porta San Pancrazio. Trenches had to be dug, coming up to the breaches made by the first attack and going on to surround the point to be taken. Once the bastions were captured, they became protected positions for the attackers and the artillery began setting up batteries there. Great quantities of earth were moved to raise the ground to the level of the ramparts,

From *Mirifiques aventures de Maître Antifer* (*Wonderful Adventures of Master Antifer*, 1894).

at the place where the curtain battery was to be constructed. That was the third time the siege batteries had moved forward.

During the nights of June 22 to 23 and June 23 to 24, work on the trenches continued, taking cover from the square, the bastions at Porta San Pancrazio, and the Vascello. On the morning of June 25, the curtain battery, armed with two sixteen-pounders and two twenty-four pounders, opened fire. But the two batteries at San Pietro in Montorio, those of the nearest bastion, and the distant but still formidable batteries at Testaccio and Sant'Alessis, returned their fire. Exposed to the shelling of five batteries, and all alone in the face of that devastating horizon of fire, the curtain battery was overwhelmed. The embrasures were blocked and they had to wait until the two bastions were armed with cannons in order to come to its assistance.

During the night of June 24 to 25, the new trench was finished. The cannonades of the Romans were terrifying and their fire was overwhelming. The battery at the far end of the first trench had to be rearmed for a fourth time in order to fire back at Testaccio and a new battery that had just been discovered on Monte Sant'Aventino, near the churches of Sant'Alessis and Santa Sabina. This was an anxious time. Would the countless projectiles of the besieged troops crush the French positions?

But now, on the morning of June 25, a negotiator appeared over the trenches, accompanied by a small group. Since no one noticed him at first, the besiegers kept up their fire and a few men fell around him. One of them was a Frenchman, the painter Laviroy, one of those brave souls who volunteer their services to every questionable cause for freedom and every rebellion in the cause of liberty. Finally the firing stopped and the negotiator was taken to headquarters. Unfortunately, no one had taken the precaution of blindfolding him, and he was able to see the new batteries under construction. In fact, that must have been the real reason why he had come, but as a pretext he was bringing a protest against the bombardment, signed by most of the consuls of Europe.

On his way through San Carlo, he passed the ranks of the engineers.

"It's him! It's still him!" shouted Henri Formont.

"Now we've got him!" roared Jean Taupin.

He was about to rush at him, but the negotiator Andreani looked at him angrily and disdainfully. Knowing that he was protected by the laws of war, he continued on his way.

"He's immune," said Annibal.

"I want to follow him, I want to see him, I want to look him in the face, so that his detestable image will be engraved in my hatred."

That was the young captain speaking. He followed the traitor, who was protected from his vengeance by the laws of war, as far as headquarters.

General Oudinot, after hearing the consuls' demands, disregarded their protest. As a loyal soldier, he knew that it was horrible to destroy a city. He knew that the bombardment was not the French way. But he was not responsible for missiles that went astray, and while he could have devastated the Trastevere under a hail of projectiles, he had confined himself to shelling the dangerous positions held by the Romans, such as the trenches and the batteries at St. Peter's.

Andreani's mission proved unsuccessful, but the double traitor had been able to observe the besiegers' preparations and take a long, hateful look at the staff captain before being led back to the outposts.

The following night, progress was made towards the highway, taking cover from the Vascello. During the day, an attempt was made to open fire a second time from the curtain battery, but it was overwhelmed again and silenced. The arming of the bastions, which had become so indispensible, was finally accomplished. The one on the right received four cannons, which were to return the fire from the batteries at the Porta San Pancrazio and St. Peter's. The one on the left had three cannons and six howitzers aimed at St. Peter's, the right-hand bastion of San Pancrazio, and Garibaldi's house. On the evening of June 26, the artillery also constructed, near the batteries at Villa Corsini, a fourteenth battery, more than two hundred meters from the square, to open a breach in the right-hand bastion of the Porta San Pancrazio, while another one, made at the beginning of the siege, would bombard the left-hand bastion. In this way, the objective was to open two new breaches, in order to mount a new assault and occupy the two bastions at the Porta San Pancrazio, thus forcing the city to capitulate. The activity had never been more intense. On the morning of June 27, thirteen batteries opened fire simultaneously. From Testaccio to St. Peter's, from the villas to the green-shuttered house, cannonballs and bombs traced out an inescapable network of fire which fell on the combatants. Several French officers were killed, but the attackers managed to put a temporary stop to the firing from St. Peter's.

The two breaches undertaken in the bastions at the Porta San Pancrazio were proceeding unevenly. The one on the right was almost large enough to permit entry, but the one on the left was not opening, because the Corsini battery could not see the base of the wall and therefore could not readily penetrate it. Most of the cannonballs grazed the top of the wall and went on to land in Rome. One of them knocked the head off a statue on the Capitole. Another went right into the Triumvirate's meeting room.

The attackers worked at making trenches during the night of June 28 to 29, moving a defensive shield ahead of them, for they were exposed to heavy fire. Nevertheless, they extended the branch tunnels right up to the breach. The Romans thought they were under attack and tried using rockets to shine a light on the French, but they did not put a stop to the work, despite their formidable fire.

The next day, the assault was put on the agenda, as follows: six elite companies, chosen from the regiments of the second division, made up two assault columns. The first was to go up to the breach, while the second remained in reserve in the side trench. A third column, made up of elite companies from the trench guards, was ready to charge from the right-hand bastion and join the first column in the bastion under attack. They would do this by crossing the terrain between the bastions and the old wall, cut by trenches and within range of the batteries at St. Peter's. Each column, made up as for the first assault, was led by an officer of the engineers. Colonel Lespinasse was placed in command of the troops, and Major Galbaud Dufort again directed the attack.

The night of June 29 to 30 finally arrived. The troops at Santa Passera were kept on the alert by some thirty fire-ships launched against the bridge, but they were able to stop them in time. General Guesvilliers made a feint through the Porta del Popolo to mislead the Romans.

At two a.m., the first column, commanded by Captain d'Austrelaine, charged the breach under heavy fire from the interior retrenchments and the Garibaldi house. They leaped into the Roman trenches, bayonetted a hundred and fifty men and took a hundred prisoners, including eighteen officers. The sappers rushed at the batteries on the Aurelian Wall and fought hand to hand with the artillerymen, several of whom were killed at their guns. Eight cannons remained in their possession. The soldiers, caught up in the excitement and intoxication of success, even advanced as far as the Porta San Pancrazio, but they were soon forced to return to the bastion that they had taken by storm. The reserve column came in with its gabions and blocked it up at the throat. The right-hand side of the bastion was next to the abandoned battery, and connected at the back to a house located at the corner of the bastion. It was while making his way to these various points to organize the work, that the valiant Major Galbaud Dufort was struck by two bullets. He was taken to the dressing station and died in Rome several days later. Command of the attack passed to Colonel Ardent. The third column rushed out of its bastion and took the Roman positions. After some hesitation, during which the attackers fired on each other, it rejoined the assault columns and the Janiculum was taken.

Nine officers and a hundred and ten soldiers lay on the field of battle. The Romans had put up a valiant defense, for the position was an important one. At four o'clock in the morning, firing resumed with renewed intensity. The prisoners were taken to headquarters and from there sent to Corsica. Around ten o'clock there was a cease-fire to bury the dead lying in the bastions. The work of trenching continued.

General Vaillant had just scored a great coup. The attackers now dominated Rome. The capture of the bastions at Porta San Pancrazio compromised the safety of the square. The French could move from house to house at will along the streets of the Trastevere, or bombard the Eternal City.

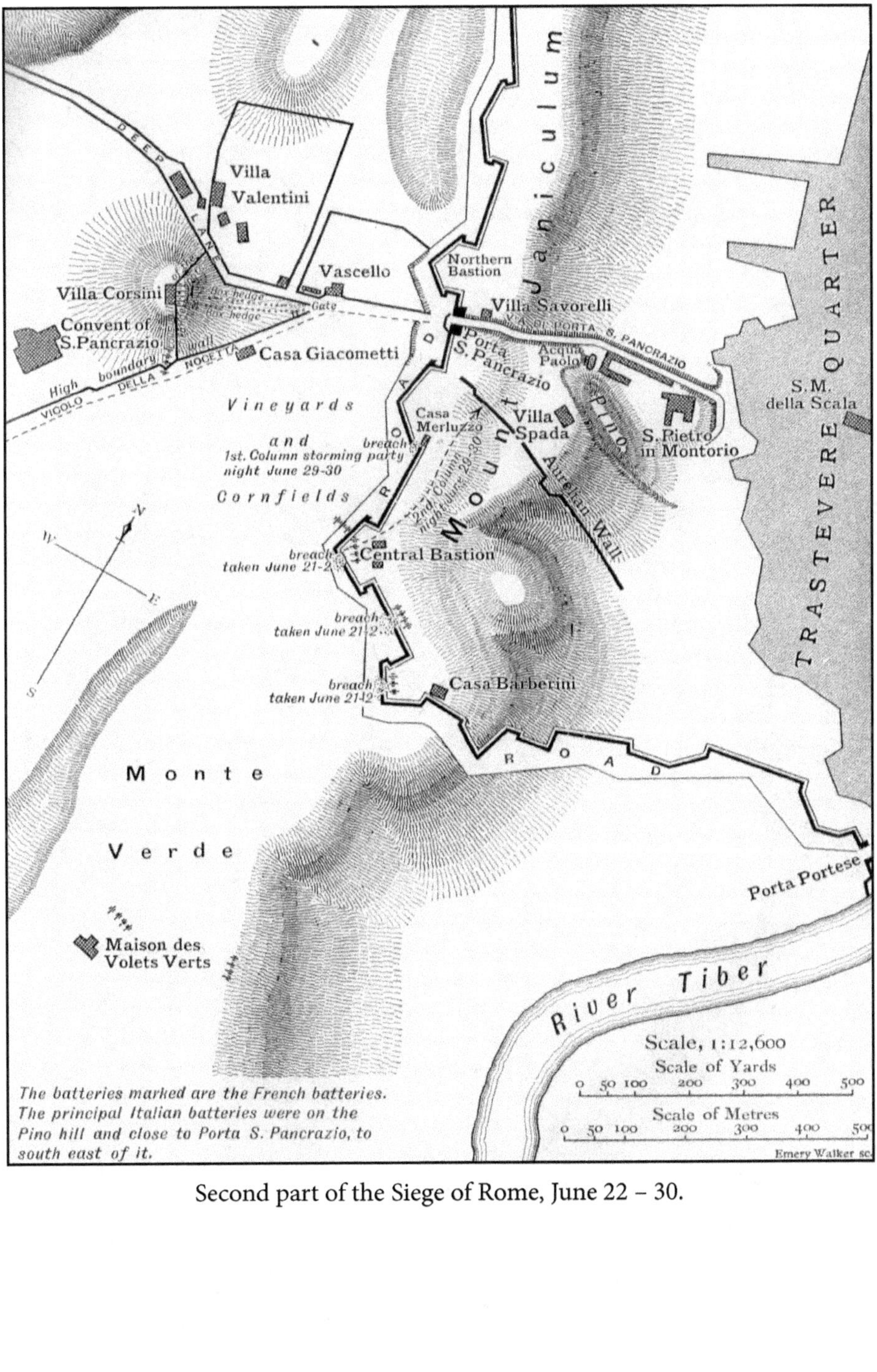

Villa
Valentini

Vascello

Northern
Bastion

Villa Corsini

Villa Savorelli

Convent of
S.Pancrazio

PORTA S. PANCRAZIO

Porta
S. Pancrazio

Acqua
Paolo

Casa Giacometti

High   boundary   wall
VICOLO   DELLA   NOCETTA

S.M.
della Scala

Vineyards

Casa
Merluzzo

Villa
Spada

S. Pietro
in Montorio

and   breach
1st. Column storming party
night June 29-30

2nd. Column
night June 29-30

Cornfields

Aurelian Wall

breach
taken June 21-2

Central Bastion

breach
taken June 21-2

breach
taken June 21-2

Casa Barberini

M o n t e

R   O   A   D

V e r d e

Porta Portese

Maison des
Volets Verts

River   Tiber

Scale, 1:12,600
Scale of Yards
0 50 100   200   300   400   500

Scale of Metres
0 50 100   200   300   400   500

The batteries marked are the French batteries.
The principal Italian batteries were on the
Pino hill and close to Porta S. Pancrazio, to
south east of it.

Emery Walker sc.

Second part of the Siege of Rome, June 22 – 30.

Chapter V

CAPITULATION AND CONCLUSION

ROME WAS IN DESPERATE STRAITS!

All the people who had no interest, either for reasons of hatred or of speculation, in winning this useless war openly called for the city's surrender. In fact, those who were fiercely conducting the defense were less Roman than the Romans themselves. General Garibaldi, who hired out his mercenaries and his revolutionary talents to every revolt and every extremist party, actively promoted the struggle. His legion, so brave, so hot-tempered, so fiery, was like St. Elmo's fire. It could only live in the midst of a storm. In peacetime it could find no employment for its bravery and loyalty. This handful of men risked their lives in everyday places, and had to get killed in order to make a living.

The triumvirs, Mazzini, Saffi, and Armellini, also stood to gain by prolonging this state of affairs. For them, victory meant power, while defeat meant decline. Despite the republicans' austerity measures, it is pleasant to sit comfortably in a position of power, and for the democrats especially, unaccustomed to luxury, the throne had a comfortable elasticity. That's the way the world goes! While true kings try to downplay their titles, while they hide and stay in the background, the ordinary leaders of an executive power wear the crown ostentatiously and act the king in every way they can. And so the triumvirs, absolute masters of the city, had sworn to defend it to the last. Since Rome was not surrounded, there would still be time to escape, to go and serve some new-born republic, or wait out events in a neutral country: in London, for example, where the government is so constitutional, so liberal, so strong, that it recently allowed an illustrious refugee to publish unhindered a book on the decline of England.[1]

The fact is that true liberty can only live under a solidly based and immovable power, a power whose stability is not at the mercy of disastrous elections or possibly successful *coups de main*. In a republic, every man can legally aspire to attain supreme power. It follows that ambitious people, who have nothing to lose and everything to gain, will be in open conflict with the powers of the day and anarchy will keep sneaking in under those popular flowers that only grow in the hothouses of revolution. And yet, government is a serious matter. The road to power is not just like going to church. Conventions, principles, prejudices, and constitutions that are the unshakeable foundations of a state may not be violated as if they were minor obstacles, simply in order to reach the goal sooner. When all mad ambitions are given complete freedom, and not held in check by the great and solid principle of heredity, which opposes their endeavors, anarchy reigns in the country, liberty is throttled by its own hand, and dictatorship comes striking heavy blows. While rioters manage to avoid their just punishment, the peaceful segment of the population is ruined in its business, its well-being, and its future.

That is what was happening in Rome. Quiet people, naturally accustomed to greater freedom, had never been less free than under the republic. They soon began to miss Pius IX and his wise institutions. The pope, incidentally, being a man of eminent merit, had realized that he would have to secularize power and not entrust it only to the priests. There are some tasks that are not appropriate for consecrated hands. To guarantee his independence in the eyes of the Catholic world, the head of the Church must be the temporal leader of his states. Without that sovereignty, he would be at the mercy of any government willing to receive him. He would be nothing more than a hired employee of a state, and religion, being no longer free, would no longer be Catholic. But the pope, as king of his own kingdom, could very well delegate the exercise of his authority to secular minds. In some cases, he had to do so. In Rome, for instance, the police force is

---

1. This "illustrious refugee" was probably Louis-Napoléon Bonaparte. He lived in London from 1838 to 1840 and went there again in 1846 after his escape from the fort at Ham. He found misery among the English working class and published numerous writings, mainly on social questions.

made up of priests, and it is very distasteful, even to the least delicate, to see them gliding along in those dark drains through which flow the impurities of an entire state. The cardinal vicar, as chief of police, commands an army of subordinates, whose clerical nature ought to keep them removed from such occult manipulations. Furthermore, the great principle of the confession no longer offers any guarantee when ministers of religion indulge, on a daily basis, in the shameful practices of denunciation and espionage. And so the pope had to set about promptly reforming all those indiscretions, which destroy a government's tact.

The Roman people understood the situation more clearly than their leaders, who had a vested interest in not understanding it. They looked back longingly on their former tranquillity. In spite of false news reports, they could see that the besiegers were advancing step by step and would soon be in control of the square. Further resistance, which would be futile anyway, might subject the Romans to the sorry necessities of war and subject their city, captured by force, to all the horrors of bombardment and pillage.

The Constituent Assembly, for its part, opened its eyes. The revolutionary movements in France, on which it had counted, were now pacified, and Louis-Napoléon Bonaparte, the President of the Republic, was already hinting that his authority would not be short-lived. After he had brought peace to the country, put down anarchy, revived commerce, restored confidence, and given the state solid and durable institutions, he was not about to let someone else enjoy the fruits of his work and his daring.

The Roman Constituent Assembly, therefore, gave ear to the people's complaints and resolved to put an end to the war. On June 30 it had a proclamation posted in Rome which ended as follows:

> *The Constituent Assembly declares that any further defense is futile and orders the triumvirate to carry out its decision.*

At six o'clock in the evening, just as the batteries were redoubling the intensity of their fire, a negotiator appeared, carrying a white flag. He was an officer of the municipal guard. He climbed over the trench and shouted, "This must stop. We surrender."

All along the line, the firing stopped. The negotiator was blind-folded and led to headquarters, where he communicated to the com-mander-in-chief the text of the proclamation posted in Rome.

Negotiations began immediately. The Roman city council left the city, went to Santucci, and tried to obtain terms, but General Oudi-not was determined to enter the city as a conqueror. The city council returned to Rome without having completed its negotiations. In view of the possibility of a breakdown, work continued on both sides. The besieged troops again organized the defence of the left-hand bastion of the Porta San Pancrazio, while Annibal and his company began set-ting up a battery to fire back at that bastion. Henri was with him. As the end of his terrible story drew near, he had recovered a little of the calm that had deserted him until then. He believed now that he would certainly conquer fate. The triumph of the French must have broken the evil spell cast on his life. France's victory was his own victory, and while two peoples had fought for their principles, two men had fought for their revenge. They had seen only themselves among the swarming masses, and the corpses lying on the ground seemed to have lost their lives in the service of their particular hatred. But Andreani was among the conquered and Henri among the conquerors.

During the night of June 30 to July 1, the connection between the fourth and fifth trenches was completed. The Porta San Pancrazio was surrounded by a trench that joined the salient of the right-hand bastion to the magnificent Vascello palace, recently abandoned by the Romans. Negotiations were still not completed on the following day.

This work around San Pancrazio continued during the night of July 1 to 2. The besieged troops retreated farther and farther, and Colo-nel Frossard of the engineers entered the Trastevere with a few troops. The houses were abandoned, and he was able to advance without op-position as far as the Tiber.

At many points, however, the Roman troops remained at their posts. The Lombards came to relieve Garibaldi's soldiers at San Pietro in Montorio. The famous adventurer hurriedly left Rome and fled into the Apennines. A brigade was sent after him, but with orders not to capture him. What would they have done with him?

During the night of July 2 to 3, the twenty-ninth night of the trenching operation, a small retrenchment was made near the Porta San Pancrazio. But the defense no longer had any leadership, and the

Roman troops continued to retreat. Andreani had disappeared two days earlier. As was his habit, he had left one evening by the Porta San Pancrazio and had not been seen since.

The Vascello is a magnificent summer palace, erected on the Corsini plateau. It can be seen off to the left, shortly before entering Rome by the Porta San Pancrazio. It had long been used by the Romans as an advance post, and was therefore devastated by a storm of cannonballs and crushed under a hail of missiles. The gardens were destroyed by retrenchments, the statues reduced to powder. The gaping walls revealed splendid frescoes. This magnificent palace symbolized in itself the ruins of war: sad, sharp ruins, blackened and shattered, so different from the ruins of time, which allow old buildings to collapse gradually on their dark and picturesque remains, still solid in their decrepitude, and put forth vast mantles of greenery and flowers. Time creates handsome, white-haired, old men. War, like devastating passions, produces nothing but worn-out young men, dying before their time.

Every evening, Andreani made his way to the subterranean passages lying beneath this palace. The exit from those gloomy cells led to a plain in the Roman countryside, far from the Vascello. The poor, mad Frenchwoman was there, entombed alive in a dark, narrow, stone cell. Every evening, like a tiger eyeing its prey to see whether there is any life left in its heart, Andreani went there to spy on the intelligence of the unfortunate woman locked up in that sickly and wasted body. Andreani's passions, which had previously been under control, had now burst out in all their fury. He had driven her mad by his despicable abduction. If he had respected her thus far, it was only because he wanted to possess her soul as well as her body, and was trying to discover some breath of reason in her.

That evening, Andreani had felt hatred rise up in his heart with a new source of irritation. His rival, his nearest enemy, had won. He sharpened the point of his dagger. For two days he had been living in the dank vaults of the ruined palace, equipped with a lantern. But this external ruin, he had now completed on the inside. Nineteen boxes of gunpowder were inserted in each of the building's pillars, and required only a spark to spread devastation and death far and wide.

Kneeling in Marie's cell, the man was plying her with senseless questions.

"Marie, can you hear me? We are alone. Wake up! Oh curses! Does she know that that Frenchman is at the city walls and will enter tomorrow as a conqueror? Marie, I'll kill you rather than give you up to him, but before I do, you mad woman, you will belong to me. Marie!"

The wretch was profaning the sacred name that escaped from his lips. The poor young woman was lying almost motionless. Sometimes a faint sign of intelligence flitted across her sickly face. Then her arms would contract in pain and her teeth would chatter. She was only eighteen years old. Taken away from her family, from happiness and love, she would die at the feet of a shameful wretch, without her mother's kiss to console her in the tomb, without her lover's hand to hold in a final embrace.

Andreani was circling her like a mad beast. Back and forth he went. She was driven mad by terror, and he by infamy. Sometimes he raised his dagger as if to strike her. Sometimes the point of his weapon was directed against himself. The idea occurred to him to bury himself under the ruins of the palace, along with the attackers who were no doubt occupying it.

And then passion went to his head, coursed through his veins. He clenched his foul fists and went up to Marie.

"Can you hear me?" he said.

"Holy Mary, who art in heaven, pray for us," murmured the girl.

"Be quiet!"

"Now and at the hour of our death."

Andreani put his hand over her mouth.

Suddenly a noise was heard in the underground passage. The mad woman stood up, as if galvanized into action. Her eyes, ears, and heart were caught up in a triple foreboding.

"Henri!" she exclaimed.

"It's him! It's still him!" replied the kidnapper.

Someone was walking near the cell, looking around, searching.

"Henri!" cried the poor mad woman again.

"Come here, my victim," roared Andreani, enfolding her in his arms.

The sound of voices grew nearer.

"This way."

"More gunpowder!"

"Be careful, lieutenant, there's some in every pillar."

"Marie is there! Marie is there!"

It was Henri. It was Annibal and his soldiers. Rummaging through the palace, they had found the gunpowder. Continuing their search, they had reached the subterranean passage and were now at the door of the cell. Henri threw himself against the door, but it did not yield to his efforts. The soldiers broke it down and Henri went in. Andreani had disappeared, but his dagger protruded from the girl's breast. She was dead, dead at last! She had died in pain, just when happy days were about to spread out around her.

"Marie!" stammered the poor young man, and he fell senseless beside her.

Andreani, however, escaped by another exit and returned to the underground passage. Jean Taupin and Annibal spotted him.

"Help us!" they shouted. "Vengeance!"

Now began a fast and winding race. Andreani was guided by the light of his lantern. Knowing all the obscure detours, he rapidly pulled ahead of them. Annibal and Jean despaired of catching up with him. A few gunshots fired at the fugitive had filled the passage with smoke and made it darker than ever. Suddenly a bright light shone in the darkness.

"Now you're doomed!" roared Andreani. He had just set fire to a previously prepared fuse and was running away.

Jean Taupin uttered an oath, but without a moment's hesitation, the brave soldier ran to the fuse and stamped it out. In another second, the traitor's horrible vengeance would have exploded.

Annibal flung himself into Jean's arms.

"Lieutenant! What about poor Henri? Let's go back to the cell."

It was empty. They went back to the palace, but their search was in vain. They found no one.

"It's fate, lieutenant, just as I told you."

Annibal was weeping. "Tomorrow," he said, "we'll search all through Rome. We'll find him."

"Maybe," said the soldier, also in tears.

Andreani had reached the countryside, and was never heard from again.

At last the negotiations were finished and Rome opened its gates unconditionally. At three o'clock on the afternoon of July 3, the French army made its entry into the city through the Porta Portese. Seeing that the war was over, the Trasteverins greeted it enthusiastically. The headquarters staff went to the French embassy and moved in triumphantly. The troops were billeted in Roman convents and palaces. The Constituent Assembly was dissolved and its meeting hall occupied by a regiment of dragoons. All the red flags adorning the Corso were pulled down.

And so, General Vaillant was the victor. By a combination of solicitude and genius, he had, to a large extent, spared the lives of his soldiers and taken the city at a point considered to be impregnable. His glory preceded by two years his distinctions and honors.

Poor Annibal searched in vain for Henri, but his friend was now only a corpse, which would be found near the pontoon bridge of Santa Passera.

Annibal repeated the words of Jean Taupin: "It's fate! It's fate!"

A week after the French entered Rome, the pontifical government was proclaimed at St. Peter's, and at the Vatican the pope's colors replaced the flag of the Italian uprising.

✛

MARTIN PAZ, or
THE PEARL OF LIMA

by Jules Verne

Translated by Anne T. Wilbur

For bibliographic information on this text, see the introduction, pages 11-12, and footnote 13.

Chapter I

THE PLAZA-MAYOR

THE SUN HAD DISAPPEARED behind the snowy peaks of the Cordilleras; but the beautiful Peruvian sky long retains, through the transparent veil of night, the reflection of his rays; the atmosphere is impregnated with a refreshing coolness, which in these burning latitudes affords freedom of breath; it is the hour in which one can live a European life, and seek without on the verandas some cooling gentle zephyr; it seems as if a metallic roof was then interposed between the sun and the earth, which, retaining the heat and suffering only the light to pass, offers beneath its shelter a reparative repose.

This much desired hour had at last sounded from the clock of the cathedral. While the earliest stars were rising above the horizon, the numerous promenaders were traversing the streets of Lima, wrapped in their light mantles, and conversing gravely on the most trivial affairs. There was a great movement of the populace on the Plaza-Mayor, that forum of the ancient city of kings; artisans were profiting by the coolness to quit their daily labors; they circulated actively among the crowd, crying their various merchandise; the ladies of Lima, carefully enveloped in the mantillas which mask their countenances, with the exception of the right eye, darted stealthy glances on the surrounding masses; they undulated through the groups of smokers, like foam at the will of the waves; other señoras, in ball costume, *coiffed* only with their abundant hair or some natural flowers, passed in large calêches, throwing on the *caballeros* nonchalant regards.

But these glances were not bestowed indiscriminately upon the young cavaliers; the thoughts of the noble ladies could rest only on aristocratic heights. The Indians passed without lifting their eyes upon them, knowing themselves to be beneath their notice; betraying by no gesture or word, the bitter envy of their hearts. They contrasted strongly with the half-breeds, or mestizoes, who, repulsed like the former, vented their indignation in cries and protestations.

The proud descendants of Pizarro marched with heads high, as in the times when their ancestors founded the city of kings; their traditional scorn rested alike on the Indians whom they had conquered, and the mestizoes, born of their relations with the natives of the New World. The Indians, on the contrary, were constantly struggling to break their chains, and cherished alike aversion toward the conquerors of the ancient empire of the Incas and their haughty and insolent descendants.

But the mestizoes, Spanish in their contempt for the Indians, and Indian in their hatred which they had vowed against the Spaniards, burned with both these vivid and impassioned sentiments.

A group of these young people stood near the pretty fountain in the centre of the Plaza-Mayor. Clad in their *poncho*, a piece of cloth or cotton in the form of a parallelogram, with an opening in the middle to give passage to the head, in large pantaloons, striped with a thousand colors, *coiffed* with broad-brimmed hats of Guayaquil straw, they were talking, declaiming, gesticulating.

"You are right, André," said a very obsequious young man, whom they called Milleflores.

This was the friend, the parasite of André Certa, a young mestizo of swarthy complexion, whose thin beard gave a singular appearance to his countenance.

André Certa, the son of a rich merchant killed in the last *émeute* of the conspirator Lafuente, had inherited a large fortune; this he freely scattered among his friends, whose humble salutations he demanded in exchange for handfuls of gold.

"Of what use are these changes in government, these eternal *pronunciamentos* which disturb Peru to gratify private ambition?" resumed André, in a loud voice; "what is it to me whether Gambarra or Santa Cruz rule, if there is no equality."

"Well said," exclaimed Milleflores, who, under the most republican government, could never have been the equal of a man of sense.

"How is it," resumed André Certa, "that I, the son of a merchant, can ride only in a calêche drawn by mules? Have not my ships brought

Amancaés, Indians, and Blacks, dealers in coconuts, beefsteak, fruits, etc.

wealth and prosperity to the country? Is not the aristocracy of piasters worth all the titles of Spain?"

"It is a shame!" resumed the young mestizo. "There is Don Fernand, who passes in his carriage drawn by two horses! Don Fernand d'Aiquillo! He has scarcely property enough to feed his coachman and horses, and he must come to parade himself proudly about the square. And, hold! here is another! the Marquis Don Vegal!"

A magnificent carriage, drawn by four fine horses, at that moment entered the Plaza-Mayor; its only occupant was a man of proud mien, mingled with sadness; he gazed, without seeming to see them, on the multitude assembled to breathe the coolness of the evening. This man was the Marquis Don Vegal, knight of Alcantara, of Malta, and of Charles III. He had a right to appear in this pompous equipage; the viceroy and the archbishop could alone take precedence of him; but this great nobleman came here from ennui and not from ostentation; his thoughts were not depicted on his countenance, they were concentrated beneath his bent brow; he received no impression from exterior objects, on which he bestowed not a look, and heard not the envious reflections of the mestizoes, when his four horses made their way through the crowd.

"I hate that man," said André Certa.

"You will not hate him long."

"I know it! All these nobles are displaying the last splendors of their luxury; I can tell where their silver and their family jewels go."

"You have not your entrée with the Jew Samuel for nothing."

"Certainly not! On his account-books are inscribed aristocratic creditors; in his strong-box are piled the wrecks of great fortunes; and in the day when the Spaniards shall be as ragged as their Cæsar de Bazan, we will have fine sport."

"Yes, we will have fine sport, dear André, mounted on your millions, on a golden pedestal! And you are about to double your fortune! When are you to marry the beautiful young daughter of old Samuel, a Limanienne to the end of her nails, with nothing Jewish about her but her name of Sarah?"

"In a month," replied André Certa, proudly, "there will be no fortune in Peru which can compete with mine."

"But why," asked some one, "do you not espouse some Spanish girl of high descent?"

"I despise these people as much as I hate them."

André Certa concealed the fact of his having been repulsed by several noble families, into which he had sought to introduce himself.

His interlocutor still wore an expression of doubt, and the brow of the mestizo had contracted, when the latter was rudely elbowed by a man of tall stature, whose gray hairs proclaimed him to be at least fifty, while the muscular force of his firmly knit limbs seemed undiminished by age.

This man was clad in a brown vest, through which appeared a coarse shirt with a broad collar; his short breeches, striped with green, were fastened by red garters to stockings of clay-color; on his feet were sandals made of *ojotas*, ox-hide prepared for this purpose; beneath his high-pointed hat gleamed large ear-rings. His complexion was dark. After having jostled André Certa, he looked at him fixedly, but with no particular expression.

"Miserable Indian!" exclaimed the mestizo, raising his hand upon him.

His companions restrained him. Milleflores, whose face was pale with terror, exclaimed:

"André! André! take care."

"A vile slave! to presume to elbow me!"

"It is a madman! it is the *Sambo*!"

The *Sambo*, as the name indicated, was an Indian of the mountains; he continued to fix his eyes on the mestizo, whom he had intentionally jostled. The latter, whose anger was unbounded, had seized a poignard at his girdle, and was about to have rushed on the impassable aggressor, when a guttural cry, like that of the *cilguero*, (a kind of linnet of Peru,) re-echoed in the midst of the tumult of promenaders, and the Sambo disappeared.

"Brutal and cowardly!" exclaimed André.

"Control yourself," said Milleflores, softly. "Let us leave the Plaza-Mayor; the Limanienne ladies are too haughty here."

Ladies of Lima on the promenade.

As he said these words, the brave Milleflores looked cautiously around to see whether he was not within reach of the foot or arm of some Indian in the neighborhood.

"In an hour, I must be at the house of Jew Samuel," said André.

"In an hour! we have time to pass to the *Calle del Peligro*; you can offer some oranges or ananas to the charming *tapadas* who promenade there. Shall we go, gentlemen?"

The group directed their steps toward the extremity of the square, and began to descend the street of Danger, where Milleflores hoped his good looks would be appreciated; but it was nightfall, and the young Limaniennes merited better than ever their name of *tapadas* (hidden), for they drew their mantles more closely over their countenances.

"You vile Indian!" the mestizo said.

The Plaza-Mayor was all alive; the cries and the tumult were re-doubled; the guards on horseback, stationed before the central portico of the viceroy's palace, situated on the north side of the square, could scarcely maintain their position amid the shifting crowd; there were merchants for all customers and customers for all merchants. The greatest variety of trades seemed to be congregated there, and from the *Portal de Escribanos* to the *Portal de Botoneros*, there was one immense display of articles of every kind, the Plaza-Mayor serving at once as promenade, bazaar, market and fair. The ground-floor of the viceroy's palace is occupied by shops; along the first story runs an immense gallery where the crowd can promenade on days of public rejoicing; on the east side of the square rises the cathedral, with its steeples and light balustrades, proudly adorning its two towers; the basement story of the edifice being ten feet high, and containing warehouses full of the products of tropical climates.

In the centre of this square is situated the beautiful fountain, con-structed in 1653, by the orders of the viceroy, the Comte de Salvatierra. From the top of the pillar, which rises in the middle of the fountain and is surmounted with a statue of Fame, the water falls in sheets, and is discharged into a basin beneath through the mouths of lions. It is here that the water-carriers (*aguadores*) load their mules with barrels, attach a bell to a hoop, and mount behind their liquid merchandise.

This square is therefore noisy from morning till evening, and when the stars of night rise above the snowy summits of the Cordilleras, the tumult of the *élite* of Lima equals the matinal hubbub of the merchants.

Nevertheless, when the *oracion* (evening *angelus*) sounds from the bell of the cathedral, all this noise suddenly ceases; to the clamor of pleasure succeeds the murmur of prayer; the women pause in their walk and put their hands on their rosaries, invoking the Virgin Mary. Then, not a merchant dares sell his merchandise, not a customer thinks of buying, and this square, so recently animated, seems to have become a vast solitude.

While the Limanians paused and knelt at the sound of the *ange-lus*, a young girl, carefully surrounded by her discreet mantle, sought to pass through the praying multitude; she was followed by a mestizo woman, a sort of duenna, who watched every glance and step. The du-enna, as if she had not understood the warning bell, continued her way

The tall young Indian, his arms crossed, was awaiting his opponent.

through the devout populace: to the general surprise succeeded harsh epithets. The young girl would have stopped, but the duenna kept on.

"Do you see that daughter of Satan?" said some one near her.

"Who is that *balarina*—that impious dancer?"

"It is one of the Carcaman women." (A reproachful name bestowed upon Europeans.)

The young girl at last stopped, blushing and confused.

Suddenly a *gaucho*, a merchant of mules, seized her by the shoulder, and would have compelled her to kneel; but he had scarcely laid his hand upon her when a vigorous arm rudely felled him to the ground. This scene, rapid as lightning, was followed by a moment of confusion.

"Save yourself, miss," said a gentle and respectful voice in the ear of the young girl.

The latter turned, pale with terror, and saw a young Indian of tall stature, who, with his arms tranquilly folded, was awaiting with firm foot the attack of his adversary.

"We are lost!" exclaimed the duenna; "*niña, niña*, let us go, for the love of God!" and she seized the arm of the young girl, who disappeared, while the crowd rose and dispersed.

The *gaucho* had risen, bruised with his fall, and thinking it not prudent to seek revenge, rejoined his mules, muttering threats.

Chapter II

Evening in the Streets of Lima

NIGHT HAD SUCCEEDED, almost without intervening twilight, the glare of day. The two women quickened their pace, for it was late; the young girl, still under the influence of strong emotion, maintained silence, while the duenna murmured some mysterious paternosters— they walked rapidly through one of the sloping streets leading from the Plaza-Mayor.

This place is situated more than four hundred feet above the level of the sea, and about a hundred and fifty rods from the bridge thrown over the river Rimac, which forms the diameter of the city of Lima, arranged in a semicircle.

The city of Lima lies in the valley of the Rimac, nine leagues from its mouth; at the north and east commence the first undulations of ground which form a part of the great chain of the Andes: the valley of Lungaucho, formed by the mountains of San Cristoval and the Aman-caës, which rise behind Lima, terminates in its suburbs. The city lies on one bank of the river; the other is occupied by the suburb of San Lazaro, and is united to the city by a bridge of five arches, the upper piers of which are triangular to break the force of the current; while the lower ones present to the promenaders circular benches, on which the fashionables may lounge during the summer evenings, and where they can contemplate a pretty cascade.

The city is two miles long from east to west, and only a mile and a quarter wide from the bridge to the walls; the latter, twelve feet in height, ten feet thick at their base, are built of *adobes*, a kind of brick dried in the sun, and made of potter's clay mingled with a great quantity of chopped straw: these walls are calculated to resist earthquakes; the enclosure, pierced with seven gates and three posterns, terminates at its south-east extremity by the little citadel of Santa Caterina.

Such is the ancient city of kings, founded in 1534 by Pizarro, on the day of Epiphany; it has been and is still the theatre of constant-ly renewed revolutions. Lima, situated three miles from the sea, was formerly the principal storehouse of America on the Pacific Ocean, thanks to its Port of Callao, built in 1779, in a singular manner. An old vessel, filled with stones, sand, and rubbish of all sorts, was wrecked on the shore; piles of the mangrove-tree, brought from Guayaquil and im-pervious to water, were driven around this as a centre, which became the immovable base on which rose the mole of Callao.

The climate, milder and more temperate than that of Carthagena or Bahia, situated on the opposite side of America, makes Lima one of the most agreeable cities of the New World: the wind has two direc-tions from which it never varies; either it blows from the south-east, and becomes cool by crossing the Pacific Ocean; or it comes from the south-west, impregnated with the mild atmosphere of the forests and the freshness which it has derived from the icy summits of the Cordil-leras.

The nights beneath tropical latitudes are very beautiful and very clear; they mysteriously prepare that beneficent dew which fertilizes a soil exposed to the rays of a cloudless sky—so the inhabitants of Lima prolong their nocturnal conversations and receptions; household la-bors are quietly finished in the dwellings refreshed by the shadows, and the streets are soon deserted; scarcely is some *pulperia* still haunt-ed by the drinkers of *chica* or *quarapo*.

These, the young girl, whom we have seen, carefully avoided; crossing in the middle of the numerous squares scattered about the city, she arrived, without interruption, at the bridge of the Rimac, lis-tening to catch the slightest sound—which her emotion exaggerated, and hearing only the bells of a train of mules conducted by its *arriero*, or the joyous *stribillo* of some Indian.

This young girl was called Sarah, and was returning to the house of the Jew Samuel, her father; she was clad in a *saya* of satin—a kind of petticoat of a dark color, plaited in elastic folds, and very narrow at the bottom, which compelled her to take short steps, and gave her that graceful delicacy peculiar to the Limanienne ladies; this petti-

View of the Plaza Mayor in Lima.

coat, ornamented with lace and flowers, was in part covered with a silk mantle, which was raised above the head and enveloped it like a hood; stockings of exquisite fineness and little satin shoes peeped out beneath the graceful *saya*; bracelets of great value encircled the arms of the young girl, whose rich toilet was of exquisite taste, and her whole person redolent of that charm so well expressed by the Spanish word *donaire*.

Milleflores might well say to André Certa that his betrothed had nothing of the Jewess but the name, for she was a faithful specimen of those admirable señoras whose beauty is above all praise.

The duenna, an old Jewess, whose countenance was expressive of avarice and cupidity, was a devoted servant of Samuel, who paid her liberally.

At the moment when these two women entered the suburb of San Lazaro, a man, clad in the robe of a monk, and with his head covered with a cowl, passed near them and looked at them attentively. This man, of tall stature, possessed a countenance expressive of gentleness and benevolence; it was Padre Joachim de Camarones; he threw a glance of intelligence on Sarah, who immediately looked at her follower.

The latter was still grumbling, muttering and whining, which prevented her seeing any thing; the young girl turned toward the good father and made a graceful sign with her hand.

"Well, señora," said the old woman, sharply, "is it not enough to have been insulted by these Christians, that you should stop to look at a priest?"

Sarah did not reply.

"Shall we see you one day, with rosary in hand, engaged in the ceremonies of the church?"

The ceremonies of the church—*las funciones de iglesia*—are the great business of the Limanian ladies.

"You make strange suppositions," replied the young girl, blushing.

"Strange as your conduct! What would my master Samuel say, if he knew what had taken place this evening?"

"Am I to blame because a brutal muleteer chose to address me?"

"I understand, señora," said the old woman, shaking her head, "and will not speak of the *gaucho*."

"Then the young man did wrong in defending me from the abuse of the populace?"

"Is it the first time the Indian has thrown himself in your way?"

The countenance of the young girl was fortunately sheltered by her mantle, for the darkness would not have sufficed to conceal her emotion from the inquisitive glance of the duenna.

"But let us leave the Indian where he is," resumed the old woman, "it is not my business to watch him. What I complain of is, that in order not to disturb these Christians, you wished to remain among them! Had you not some desire to kneel with them? Ah, señora, your father would soon dismiss me if I were guilty of such apostasy."

But the young girl no longer heard; the remark of the old woman on the subject of the young Indian had inspired her with sweeter thoughts; it seemed to her that the intervention of this young man was providential; and she turned several times to see if he had not followed her in the shadow. Sarah had in her heart a certain natural confidence which became her wonderfully; she felt herself to be the child of these warm latitudes, which the sun decorates with surprising vegetation; proud as a Spaniard, if she had fixed her regards on this man, it was because he had stood proudly in the presence of her pride, and had not begged a glance as a reward of his protection.

In imagining that the Indian was near her, Sarah was not mistaken; Martin Paz, after having come to the assistance of the young girl, wished to ensure her safe retreat; so when the promenaders had dispersed, he followed her, without being perceived by her, but without concealing himself; the darkness alone favoring his pursuit.

This Martin Paz was a handsome young man, wearing with unparalleled nobility the national costume of the Indian of the mountains; from his broad-brimmed straw hat escaped fine black hair, whose curls harmonized with the bronze of his manly face. His eyes shone with infinite sweetness, like the transparent atmosphere of starry nights; his well-formed nose surmounted a pretty mouth, unlike that of most of his race. He was one of the noblest descendants of Manco-Capac, and his veins were full of that ardent blood which leads men to the accomplishment of lofty deeds.

He was proudly draped in his *poncho* of brilliant colors; at his girdle hung one of those Malay poignards, so terrible in a practiced hand, for they seem to be riveted to the arm which strikes. In North America, on the shores of Lake Ontario, Martin Paz would have been a great chief among those wandering tribes which have fought with the English so many heroic combats.

Martin Paz knew that Sarah was the daughter of the wealthy Samuel; he knew her to be the most charming woman in Lima; he knew her to be betrothed to the opulent mestizo André Certa; he knew that by her birth, her position and her wealth she was beyond the reach of his heart; but he forgot all these impossibilities in his all-absorbing passion. It seemed to him that this beautiful young girl belonged to him, as the llama to the Peruvian forests, as the eagle to the depths of immensity.

Plunged in his reflections, Martin Paz hastened his steps to see the *saya* of the young girl sweep the threshold of the paternal dwelling; and Sarah herself, half-opening then her mantilla, cast on him a bewildering glance of gratitude.

He was quickly joined by two Indians of the species of *zambos*, pillagers and robbers, who walked beside him.

"Martin Paz," said one of them to him, "you ought this very evening to meet our brethren in the mountains."

"I shall be there," coldly replied the other.

"The schooner *Annonciation* has appeared in sight from Callao, tacked for a few moments, then, protected by the point, rapidly disappeared. She will undoubtedly approach the land near the mouth of the Rimac, and our bark canoes must be there to relieve her of her merchandise. We shall need your presence."

"You are losing time by your observations. Martin Paz knows his duty and he will do it."

"It is in the name of the Sambo that we speak to you here."

"It is in my own name that I speak to you."

"Do you not fear that he will find your presence in the suburb of San Lazaro at this hour unaccountable?"

"I am where my fancy and my will have brought me."

"Before the house of the Jew?"

"Those of my brethren who are disposed to find fault can meet me to-night in the mountain."

The eyes of the three men sparkled, and this was all. The *zambos* regained the bank of the Rimac, and the sound of their footsteps died away in the darkness.

Martin Paz had hastily approached the house of the Jew. This house, like all those of Lima, had but two stories; the ground floor, built of bricks, was surmounted with walls formed of canes tied together and covered with plaster; all this part of the building, constructed to resist earthquakes, imitated, by a skillful painting, the bricks of the lower story; the square roof, called *asoetas*, was covered with flowers, and formed a terrace full of perfumes and pretty points of view.

A vast gate, placed between two pavilions, gave access to a court; but as usual, these pavilions had no window opening upon the street.

The clock of the parish church was striking eleven when Martin Paz stopped before the dwelling of Sarah. Profound silence reigned around; a flickering light within proved that the saloon of the Jew Samuel was still occupied.

Why does the Indian stand motionless before these silent walls? The cool atmosphere woos him with its transparency and its perfumes; the radiant stars send down upon the sleeping earth rays of diaphanous mildness; the white constellations illumine the darkness with their enchanting light; his heart believes in those sympathetic communications which brave time and distance.

A white form appears upon the terrace amid the flowers to which night has only left a vague outline, without diminishing their delicious

"Is it the first time that you met this young Indian?"

perfumes; the dahlias mingle with the mentzelias, with the helianthus, and, beneath the occidental breeze, form a waving basket which surrounds Sarah, the young and beautiful Jewess.

Martin Paz involuntarily raises his hands and clasps them with adoration. Suddenly the white form sinks down, as if terrified.

Martin Paz turns, and finds himself face to face with André Certa.

"Since when do the Indians pass their nights in contemplation?"

André Certa spoke angrily.

"Since the Indians have trodden the soil of their ancestors."

"Have they no longer, on the mountain side, some *yaravis* to chant, some *boleros* to dance with the girls of their caste?"

"The *cholos*," replied the Indian, in a high voice, "bestow their devotion where it is merited; the Indians love according to their hearts."

André Certa became pale with anger; he advanced a step toward his immovable rival.

"Wretch! will you quit this place?"

"Rather quit it yourself," shouted Martin Paz; and two poignards gleamed in the two right hands of the adversaries; they were of equal stature, they seemed of equal strength, and the lightnings of their eyes were reflected in the steel of their arms.

André Certa rapidly raised his arm, which he dropped still more quickly. But his poignard had encountered the Malay poignard of the Indian; at the fire which flashed from this shock, André saw the arm of Martin Paz suspended over his head, and immediately rolled on the earth, his arm pierced through.

"Help, help!" he exclaimed.

Indian priest with poncho.

The door of the Jew's house opened at his cries. Some mestizoes ran from a neighboring house; some pursued the Indian, who fled rapidly; others raised the wounded man. He had swooned.

"Who is this man?" said one of them. "If he is a sailor, take him to the hospital of Spiritu Santo; if an Indian, to the hospital of Santa Anna."

An old man advanced toward the wounded youth; he had scarcely looked upon him when he exclaimed:

"Let the poor young man be carried into my house. This is a strange mischance."

This man was the Jew Samuel; he had just recognized the betrothed of his daughter.

Martin Paz, thanks to the darkness and the rapidity of his flight, may hope to escape his pursuers; he has risked his life; an Indian assassin of a mestizo! If he can gain the open country he is safe, but he knows that the gates of the city are closed at eleven o'clock in the evening, not to be re-opened till four in the morning.

He reaches at last the stone bridge which he had already crossed. The Indians, and some soldiers who had joined them, pursue him closely; he springs upon the bridge. Unfortunately a patrol appears at the opposite extremity; Martin Paz can neither advance nor retrace his steps; without hesitation he clears the parapet and leaps into the rapid current which breaks against the corners of the stones.

The pursuers spring upon the banks below the bridge to seize the swimmer at his landing.

But it is in vain; Martin Paz does not re-appear.

Chapter III

THE JEW EVERYWHERE A JEW*

ANDRÉ CERTA, ONCE INTRODUCED into the house of Samuel, and laid in a bed hastily prepared, recovered his senses and pressed the hand of the old Jew. The physician, summoned by one of the domestics, was promptly in attendance. The wound appeared to be a slight one; the shoulder of the mestizo had been pierced in such a manner that the steel had only glided among the flesh. In a few days, André Certa might be once more upon his feet.

When Samuel was left alone with André, the latter said to him:

"You would do well to wall up the gate which leads to your terrace, Master Samuel."

"What fear you, André?"

"I fear lest Sarah should present herself there to the contemplation of the Indians. It was not a robber who attacked me; it was a rival, from whom I have escaped but by miracle!"

"By the holy tables, it is a task to bring up young girls!" exclaimed the Jew. "But you are mistaken, señor," he resumed, "Sarah will be a dutiful spouse. I spare no pains that she may do you honor."

André Certa half raised himself on his elbow.

* See the Introduction, pages 13-15, for a discussion of 19th century anti-semitism and this story. While the stereotypes in *Martin Paz* make it the most problematic of the three stories in this volume, it was the only one to be published during Verne's lifetime, appearing in both periodical and book form in French and English. By contrast, "San Carlos" and *The Siege of Rome*, which offer no objectionable aspects from today's perspective, only appeared posthumously, and this fact highlights the change in standards for the treatment of ethnicity and religion since the 19th century.

"Master Samuel, there is one thing which you do not enough re-member, that I pay you for the hand of Sarah a hundred thousand piasters."

"Señor," replied the Jew, with a miserly chuckle, "I remember it so well, that I am ready now to exchange this receipt for the money."

As he said this, Samuel drew from his pocket-book a paper which André Certa repulsed with his hand.

"The bargain is not complete until Sarah has become my wife, and she will never be such if her hand is to be disputed by such an adver-sary. You know, Master Samuel, what is my object; in espousing Sarah, I wish to be the equal of this nobility which casts such scornful glances upon us."

"Move away," replied the old man strictly.

"And you will, señor, for you see the proudest grandees of Spain throng our saloons, around the pearl of Lima."

"Where has Sarah been this evening?"

"To the Israelitish temple, with old Ammon."

"Why should Sarah attend your religious rites?"

"I am a Jew, señor," replied Samuel proudly, "and would Sarah be my daughter if she did not fulfill the duties of my religion?"

The old Jew remained sad and silent for several minutes. His bent brow rested on one of his withered hands. His face usually bronze, was now almost pale; beneath a brown cap appeared locks of an indescribable color. He was clad in a sort of great-coat fastened around the waist.

This old man trafficked every where and in every thing; he might have been a descendant of the Judas who sold his Master for thirty pieces of silver. He had been a resident of Lima ten years; his taste and his economy had led him to choose his dwelling at the extremity of the suburb of San Lazaro, and from thence he entered into various speculations to make money. By degrees, Samuel assumed a luxury uncommon in misers; his house was sumptuously furnished; his numerous domestics, his splendid equipages betokened immense revenues. Sarah was then eight years of age. Already graceful and charming, she pleased all, and was the idol of the Jew. All her inclinations were unhesitatingly gratified. Always elegantly dressed, she attracted the eyes of the most fastidious, of which her father seemed strangely careless. It will readily be understood how the mestizo, André Certa, became enamored of the beautiful Jewess. What would have appeared inexplicable to the public, was the hundred thousand piasters, the price of her hand; but this bargain was secret. And besides, Samuel trafficked in sentiments as in native productions. A banker, usurer, merchant, shipowner, he had the talent to do business with everybody. The schooner *Annonciation*, which was hovering about the mouth of the Rimac, belonged to the Jew Samuel.

Amid this life of business and speculation this man fulfilled the duties of his religion with scrupulous punctuality; his daughter had been carefully instructed in the Israelitish faith and practices.

So, when the mestizo had manifested his displeasure on this subject, the old man remained mute and pensive, and André Certa broke the silence, saying:

"Do you forget that the motive for which I espouse Sarah will compel her to become a convert to Catholicism? It is not my fault," added the mestizo; "but in spite of you, in spite of me, in spite of herself, it will be so."

"You are right," said the Jew sadly; "but, by the Bible, Sarah shall be a Jewess as long as she is my daughter."

At this moment the door of the chamber opened, and the major-domo of the Jew Samuel respectfully entered.

"Is the murderer arrested?" asked the old man.

"We have reason to believe he is dead!"

"Dead!" repeated André, with a joyful exclamation.

"Caught between us and a company of soldiers," replied the major-domo, "he was obliged to leap over the parapet of the bridge."

"He has thrown himself into the Rimac!" exclaimed André.

"And how do you know that he has not reached the shore?" asked Samuel.

"The melting of the snow has made the current rapid at that spot; besides, we stationed ourselves on each side of the river, and he did not re-appear. I have left sentinels who will pass the night in watching the banks."

"It is well," said the old man; "he has met with a just fate. Did you recognize him in his flight?"

"Perfectly, sir; it was Martin Paz, the Indian of the mountains."

"Has this man been observing Sarah for some time past?"

"I do not know," replied the servant.

"Summon old Ammon."

The major-domo withdrew.

"These Indians," said the old man, "have secret understandings among themselves; I must know whether the pursuit of this man dates from a distant period."

The duenna entered, and remained standing before her master.

"Does my daughter," asked Samuel, "know any thing of what has taken place this morning?"

"When the cries of your servants awoke me, I ran to the chamber of the señora, and found her almost motionless and of a mortal paleness."

"Fatality!" said Samuel; "continue," added he, seeing that the mestizo was apparently asleep.

Sarah on a ride with her slave Liberia; farmer, herb dealer, servant, owner.

"To my urgent inquiries as to the cause of her agitation, the señora would not reply; she retired without accepting my services, and I withdrew."

"Has this Indian often thrown himself in her way?"

"I do not know, master; nevertheless I have often met him in the streets of San Lazaro."

"And you have told me nothing of this?"

"He came to her assistance this evening on the Plaza-Mayor," added the old duenna.

"Her assistance! how?"

The old woman related the scene with downcast head.

"Ah! my daughter wishes to kneel among these Christians!" exclaimed the Jew, angrily; "and I knew nothing of all this! You deserve that I should dismiss you."

The duenna went out of the room in confusion.

"Do you not see that the marriage should take place soon?" said André Certa. "I am not asleep, Master Samuel! But I need rest, now, and I will dream of our espousals."

At these words, the old man slowly retired. Before regaining his room, he wished to assure himself of the condition of his daughter, and softly entered the chamber of Sarah.

The young girl was in an agitated slumber, in the midst of the rich silk drapery around her; a watch-lamp of alabaster, suspended from the arabesques of the ceiling, shed its soft light upon her beautiful countenance; the half-open window admitted, through lowered blinds, the quiet coolness of the air, impregnated with the penetrating perfumes of the aloes and magnolia; creole luxury was displayed in the thousand objects of art which good taste and grace had dispersed on richly carved *étagères*; and, beneath the vague and placid rays of night, it seemed as if the soul of the child was sporting amid these wonders.

The old man approached the bed of Sarah: he bent over her to listen. The beautiful Jewess seemed disturbed by sorrowful thoughts, and more than once the name of Martin Paz escaped her lips.

Samuel regained his chamber, uttering maledictions.

At the first rays of morning, Sarah hastily arose. Liberta, a full-blooded Indian attached to her service, hastened to her; and, in pursuance of her orders, saddled a mule for his mistress and a horse for himself.

Sarah was accustomed to take morning-rides, accompanied by this Indian, who was entirely devoted to her.

She was clad in a *saya* of a brown color, and a mantle of cashmere with long tassels; her head was not covered with the usual hood, but sheltered beneath the broad brim of a straw hat, which left her long black tresses to float over her shoulders; and to conceal any unusual pre-occupation, she held between her lips a *cigarette* of perfumed tobacco.

Liberta, clad like an Indian of the mountains, prepared to accompany his mistress.

"Liberta," said the young girl to him, "remember to be blind and dumb."

Once in the saddle, Sarah left the city as usual, and began to ride through the country; she directed her way toward Callao. The port was in full animation: there had been a conflict during the night between the revenue-officers and a schooner, whose undecided movements betrayed a fraudulent speculation. The *Annonciation* seemed to have been awaiting some suspicious barks near the mouth of the Rimac; but before the latter could reach her, she had been compelled to flee before the custom-house boats, which had boldly given her chase.

Various rumors were in circulation respecting the destination of this vessel—which bore no name on her stern. According to some, this schooner, laden with Colombian troops, was seeking to seize the principal vessels of Callao; for Bolivar had it in his heart to revenge the affront given to the soldiers left by him in Peru, and who had been driven from it in disgrace.

She knelt and prayed for the soul of Martin Paz.

According to others, the schooner was simply a smuggler of European goods.

Without troubling herself about these rumors, more or less important, Sarah, whose ride to the port had been only a pretext, returned toward Lima, which she reached near the banks of the Rimac.

She ascended them toward the bridge: numbers of soldiers, mestizoes, and Indians, were stationed at various points on the shore.

Liberta had acquainted the young girl with the events of the night. In compliance with her orders, he interrogated some Indians leaning over the parapet, and learned that although Martin Paz had been undoubtedly drowned, his body had not yet been recovered.

Sarah was pale and almost fainting; it required all her strength of soul not to abandon herself to her grief.

Among the people wandering on the banks, she remarked an Indian with ferocious features—the Sambo! He was crouched on the bank, and seemed a prey to despair.

As Sarah passed near the old mountaineer, she heard these words, full of gloomy anger:

"Wo! wo! They have killed the son of the Sambo! They have killed my son!"

The young girl resolutely drew herself up, made a sign to Liberta to follow her; and this time, without caring whether she was observed or not, went directly to the church of Santa Anna; left her mule in charge of the Indian, entered the Catholic temple, and asking for the good Father Joachim, knelt on the stone steps, praying to Jesus and Mary for the soul of Martin Paz.

Chapter IV

A SPANISH GRANDEE

ANY OTHER THAN THE INDIAN, Martin Paz, would have, indeed, perished in the waters of the Rimac; to escape death, his surprising strength, his insurmountable will, and especially his sublime coolness, one of the privileges of the free hordes of the *pampas* of the New World, had all been found necessary.

Martin knew that his pursuers would concentrate their efforts to seize him below the bridge; it seemed impossible for him to overcome the current, and that the Indian must be carried down; but by vigorous strokes he succeeded in stemming the torrent; he dived repeatedly, and finding the under-currents less strong, at last ventured to land, and concealed himself behind a thicket of mangrove-trees.

But what was to become of him? Retreat was perilous; the soldiers might change their plans and ascend the river; the Indian must then inevitably be captured; he would lose his life, and, worse yet, Sarah. His decision was rapidly made; through the narrow streets and deserted squares he plunged into the heart of the city; but it was important that he should be supposed dead; he therefore avoided being seen, since his garments, dripping with water and covered with sea-weed, would have betrayed him.

To avoid the indiscreet glances of some belated inhabitants, Martin Paz was obliged to pass through one of the widest streets of the city; a house still brilliantly illuminated presented itself: the *port-cochere* was open to give passage to the elegant equipages which were issuing from the court, and conveying to their respective dwellings the nobles of the Spanish aristocracy.

151

The Indian adroitly glided into this magnificent dwelling; he could not remain in the street, where curious *zambos* were thronging around, attracted by the carriages. The gates of the hotel were soon carefully closed, and the Indian found flight impossible.

Some lacqueys were going to and fro in the court; Martin Paz rapidly passed up a rich stairway of cedar-wood, ornamented with valuable tapestry; the saloons, still illuminated, presented no convenient place of refuge; he crossed them with the rapidity of lightning, and disappeared in a room filled with protecting darkness.

The last lustres were quickly extinguished, and the house became profoundly silent.

The Indian Paz, as a man of energy to whom moments are precious, hastened to reconnoitre the place, and to find the surest means of evasion; the windows of this chamber opened on an interior garden; flight was practicable, and Martin Paz was about to spring from them, when he heard these words:

"Señor, you have forgotten to take the diamonds which I had left on that table!"

Martin Paz turned. A man of noble stature and of great pride of countenance was pointing to a jewel-case.

At this insult Martin Paz laid his hand on his poignard. He approached the Spaniard, who stood unmoved, and, in a first impulse of indignation, raised his arm to strike him; but turning his weapon against himself, said, in a deep tone,

"Señor, if you repeat such words, I will kill myself at your feet."

The Spaniard, astonished, looked at the Indian more attentively, and through his tangled and dripping locks perceived so lofty a frankness, that he felt a strange sympathy fill his heart. He went toward the window, gently closed it, and returned toward the Indian, whose poignard had fallen to the ground.

"Who are you?" said he to him.

"The Indian, Martin Paz. I am pursued by soldiers for having defended myself against a mestizo who attacked me, and levelled him to the ground with a blow from my poignard. This mestizo is the betrothed of a young girl whom I love. Now, señor, you can deliver me to my enemies, if you judge it noble and right."

"Sir," replied the Spaniard, gravely, "I depart to-morrow for the Baths of Chorillos; if you please to accompany me, you will be for the present safe from pursuit, and will never have reason to complain of the hospitality of the Marquis Don Vegal."

Martin Paz bent coldly without manifesting any emotion.

"You can rest until morning on this bed," resumed Don Vegal; "no one here will suspect your retreat. Good-night, señor!"

The Spaniard went out of the room, and left the Indian, moved to tears by a confidence so generous; he yielded himself entirely to the protection of the marquis, and without thinking that his slumbers might be taken advantage of to seize him, slept with peaceful security.

The next day, at sunrise, the marquis gave the last orders for his departure, and summoned the Jew Samuel to come to him; in the meantime he attended the morning mass.

This was a custom generally observed by the aristocracy. From its very foundation Lima had been essentially Catholic. Besides its numerous churches, it numbered twenty-two convents, seventeen monasteries, and four *beaterios*, or houses of retreat for females who did not take the vows. Each of these establishments possessed a chapel, so that there were at Lima more than a hundred edifices for worship, where eight hundred secular or regular priests, three hundred *religieuses*, lay-brothers and sisters, performed the duties of religion.

As Don Vegal entered the church of Santa Anna, he noticed a young girl kneeling in prayer and in tears. There was so much of grief in her depression, that the marquis could not look at her without emotion; and he was preparing to console her by some kind words, when Father Joachim de Camarones approached him, saying in a low voice:

"Señor Don Vegal, pray do not approach her."

Then he made a sign to Sarah, who followed him to an obscure and deserted chapel.

Don Vegal directed his steps to the altar and listened to the mass; then, as he was returning, he thought involuntarily of the deep sadness of the kneeling maiden. Her image followed him to his hotel, and remained deeply engraven in his soul.

Don Vegal found in his saloon the Jew Samuel, who had come in compliance with his request. Samuel seemed to have forgotten the events of the night; the hope of gain animated his countenance with a natural gayety.

"What is your lordship's will?" asked he of the Spaniard.

"I must have thirty thousand piasters within an hour."

"The day will come when my brothers will rise up."

"Thirty thousand piasters! And who has them! By the holy king David, my lord, I am far from being able to furnish such a sum."

"Here are some jewels of great value," resumed Don Vegal, without noticing the language of the Jew; "besides I can sell you at a low price a considerable estate near Cusco."

"Ah! señor, lands ruin us—we have not arms enough left to cultivate them; the Indians have withdrawn to the mountains, and our harvests do not pay us for the trouble they cost."

"At what value do you estimate these diamonds?"

Samuel drew from his pocket a little pair of scales and began to weigh the stones with scrupulous skill. As he did this, he continued to talk, and, as was his custom, depreciated the pledges offered him.

"Diamonds! a poor investment! What would they bring? One might as well bury money! You will notice, señor, that this is not of the purest water. Do you know that I do not find a ready market for these costly ornaments? I am obliged to send such merchandise to the United Provinces! The Americans would buy them, undoubtedly, but to give them up to the sons of Albion. They wish besides, and it is very just, to gain an honest percentage, so that the depreciation falls upon me. I think that ten thousand piasters should satisfy your lordship. It is little, I know; but—"

"Have I not said," resumed the Spaniard, with a sovereign air of scorn, "that ten thousand piasters would not suffice?"

"Señor, I cannot give you a half real more!"

"Take away these caskets and bring me the sum I ask for. To complete the thirty thousand piasters which I need, you will take a mortgage on this house. Does it seem to you to be solid?"

"Ah, señor, in this city, subject to earthquakes, one knows not who lives or dies, who stands or falls."

And, as he said this, Samuel let himself fall on his heels several times to test the solidity of the floors.

"Well, to oblige your lordship, I will furnish you with the required sum; although, at this moment I ought not to part with money; for I am about to marry my daughter to the *caballero* André Certa. Do you know him, sir?"

"I do not know him, and I beg of you to send me this instant, the sum agreed upon. Take away these jewels."

"Will you have a receipt for them?" asked the Jew.

Don Vegal passed into the adjoining room, without replying.

"Proud Spaniard!" muttered Samuel, "I will crush thy insolence, as I disperse thy riches! By Solomon! I am a skillful man, since my interests keep pace with my sentiments."

Don Vegal, on leaving the Jew, had found Martin Paz in profound dejection of spirits, mingled with mortification.

"What is the matter?" he asked affectionately.

"Señor, it is the daughter of the Jew whom I love."

"A Jewess!" exclaimed Don Vegal, with disgust.

But seeing the sadness of the Indian, he added:

"Let us go, *amigo*, we will talk of these things afterward!"

An hour later, Martin Paz, clad in Spanish costume, left the city, accompanied by Don Vegal, who took none of his people with him.

The Baths of Chorillos are situated at two leagues from Lima. This Indian parish possesses a pretty church; during the hot season it is the rendezvous of the fashionable Limanian society. Public games, interdicted at Lima, are permitted at Chorillos during the whole summer. The señoras there display unwonted ardor, and, in decorating himself for these pretty partners, more than one rich cavalier has seen his fortune dissipated in a few nights.

Chorillos was still little frequented; so Don Vegal and Martin Paz retired to a pretty cottage, built on the sea-shore, could live in quiet contemplation of the vast plains of the Pacific Ocean.

The Marquis Don Vegal, belonging to one of the most ancient families of Peru, saw about to terminate in himself the noble line of which he was justly proud; so his countenance bore the impress of profound sadness. After having mingled for some time in political affairs, he had felt an inexpressible disgust for the incessant revolutions brought about to gratify personal ambition; he had withdrawn into a sort of solitude, interrupted only at rare intervals by the duties of strict politeness.

His immense fortune was daily diminishing. The neglect into which his vast domains had fallen for want of laborers, had compelled him to borrow at a disadvantage; but the prospect of approaching mediocrity did not alarm him; that carelessness natural to the Spanish race, joined to the ennui of a useless existence, had rendered him insensible to the menaces of the future. Formerly the husband of an adored wife, the father of a charming little girl, he had seen himself deprived, by a horrible event, of both these objects of his love. Since then, no bond of affection had attached him to earth, and he suffered his life to float at the will of events.

Don Vegal had thought his heart to be indeed dead, when he felt it palpitate at contact with that of Martin Paz. This ardent nature awoke fire beneath the ashes; the proud bearing of the Indian suited the chivalric hidalgo; and then, weary of the Spanish nobles, in whom he no longer had confidence, disgusted with the selfish mestizoes, who wished to aggrandize themselves at his expense, he took a pleasure in turning to that primitive race, who have disputed so valiantly the American soil with the soldiers of Pizarro.

According to the intelligence received by the marquis, the Indian passed for dead at Lima; but, looking on his attachment for the Jewess as worse than death itself, the Spaniard resolved doubly to save his guest, by leaving the daughter of Samuel to marry André Certa.

While Martin Paz felt an infinite sadness pervade his heart, Don Vegal avoided all allusion to the past, and conversed with the young Indian on indifferent subjects.

Meanwhile, one day, saddened by his gloomy preoccupations, the Spaniard said to him:

"Why, my friend, do you lower the nobility of your nature by a sentiment so much beneath you? Was not that bold Manco-Capac, whom his patriotism placed in the rank of heroes, your ancestor? There is a noble part left for a valiant man, who will not suffer himself to be overcome by an unworthy passion. Have you no heart to regain your independence?"

"Who is that beautiful lady?"

"We are laboring for this, señor," said the Indian; "and the day when my brethren shall rise *en masse* is perhaps not far distant."

"I understand you; you allude to the war for which your brethren are preparing among their mountains; at a signal they will descend on the city, arms in hand—and will be conquered as they have always been! See how your interests will disappear amid these perpetual revolutions of which Peru is the theatre, and which will ruin it entirely, Indians and Spaniards, to the profit of the mestizoes, who are neither."

"We will save it ourselves," exclaimed Martin Paz.

"Yes, you will save it if you understand how to play your part! Listen to me, Paz, you whom I love from day to day as a son! I say it with grief; but, we Spaniards, the degenerate sons of a powerful race, no longer have the energy necessary to elevate and govern a state. It is therefore yours to triumph over that unhappy Americanism, which tends to reject European colonization. Yes, know that only European emigration can save the old Peruvian empire. Instead of this intestine war which tends to exclude all castes, with the exception of one, frankly extend your hands to the industrious population of the Old World."

"The Indians, señor, will always see in strangers an enemy, and will never suffer them to breathe with impunity the air of their mountains. The kind of dominion which I exercise over them will be without effect on the day when I do not swear death to their oppressors, whoever they may be! And, besides, what am I now?" added Martin Paz, with great sadness; "a fugitive who would not have three hours to live in the streets of Lima."

"Paz, you must promise me that you will not return thither."

"How can I promise you this, Don Vegal? I speak only the truth, and I should perjure myself were I to take an oath to that effect."

Don Vegal was silent. The passion of the young Indian increased from day to day; the marquis trembled to see him incur certain death by re-appearing at Lima. He hastened by all his desires, he would have hastened by all his efforts, the marriage of the Jewess!

To ascertain himself the state of things he quitted Chorillos one morning, returned to the city, and learned that André Certa had recovered from his wound. His approaching marriage was the topic of general conversation.

Don Vegal wished to see this woman whose image troubled the mind of Martin Paz. He repaired, at evening, to the Plaza-Mayor. The crowd was always numerous there. There he met Father Joachim de Camarones, his confessor and his oldest friend; he acquainted him with his mode of life. What was the astonishment of the good father to learn the existence of Martin Paz. He promised Don Vegal to watch also himself over the young Indian, and to convey to the marquis any intelligence of importance.

Suddenly the glances of Don Vegal rested on a young girl, enveloped in a black mantle, reclining in a calêche.

"Who is that beautiful person?" asked he of the father.

"It is the betrothed of André Certa, the daughter of the Jew Samuel."

"She! the daughter of the Jew!"

The marquis could hardly suppress his astonishment, and, pressing the hand of Father Joachim, pensively took the road to Chorillos.

He had just recognized in Sarah, the pretended Jewess, the young girl whom he had seen praying with such Christian fervor, at the church of Santa Anna.

Chapter V

THE HATRED OF THE INDIANS

SINCE THE COLOMBIAN TROOPS, confided by Bolivar to the orders of General Santa Cruz, had been driven from lower Peru, this country, which had been incessantly agitated by *pronunciamentos*, military revolts, had recovered some calmness and tranquillity.

In fact, private ambition no longer had any thing to expect; the president Gambarra seemed immovable in his palace of the Plaza-Mayor. In this direction there was nothing to fear; but the true danger, concealed, imminent, was not from these rebellions, as promptly extinguished as kindled, and which seemed to flatter the taste of the Americans for military parades.

This unknown peril escaped the eyes of the Spaniards, too lofty to perceive it, and the attention of the mestizoes, who never wished to look beneath them.

And yet there was an unusual agitation among the Indians of the city; they often mingled with the *serranos*, the inhabitants of the mountains; these people seemed to have shaken off their natural apathy. Instead of rolling themselves in their *ponchos*, with their feet turned to the spring sun, they were scattered throughout the country, stopping one another, exchanging private signals, and haunting the least frequented *pulperias*, in which they could converse without danger.

This movement was principally to be observed on one of the squares remote from the centre of the city. At the corner of a street stood a house, of only one story, whose wretched appearance struck the eye disagreeably.

A tavern of the lowest order, a *chingana*, kept by an old Indian woman, offered to the lowest *zambos* the *chica*, beer of fermented maize, and the *quarapo*, a beverage made of the sugar-cane.

The concourse of Indians on this square took place only at certain hours, and principally when a long pole was raised on the roof of the inn as a signal of assemblage, then the *zambos* of every profession, the *capataz*, the *arrieros*, muleteers, the *carreteros*, carters, entered the *chingana*, one by one, and immediately disappeared in the great hall; the *padrona* (hostess) seemed very busy, and leaving to her servant the care of the shop, hastened to serve herself her usual customers.

A few days after the disappearance of Martin Paz, there was a numerous assembly in the hall of the inn; one could scarcely through the darkness, rendered still more obscure by the tobacco-smoke, distinguish the frequenters of this tavern. Fifty Indians were ranged around a long table; some were chewing the *coca*, a kind of tea-leaf, mingled with a little piece of fragrant earth called *manubi*; others were drinking from large pots of fermented maize; but these occupations did not distract their attention, and they were closely listening to the speech of an Indian.

This was the Sambo, whose fixed eyes were strangely wild. He was clad as on the Plaza-Mayor.

After having carefully observed his auditors, the Sambo commenced in these terms:

"The children of the Sun can converse on grave affairs; there is no perfidious ear to hear them; on the square, some of our friends, disguised as street-singers, will attract the attention of the passers-by, and we shall enjoy entire liberty."

In fact the tones of a mandoline and of a *viguela* were echoing without.

The Indians within, knowing themselves in safety, lent therefore close attention to the words of the Sambo, in whom they placed entire confidence.

"What news can the Sambo give us of Martin Paz?" asked an Indian.

"None—is he dead or not? The Great Spirit only knows. I am expecting some of our brethren, who have descended the river to its mouth, perhaps they will have found the body of Martin Paz."

"He was a good chief," said Manangani, a ferocious Indian, much dreaded; "but why was he not at his post on the day when the schooner brought us arms?"

The Sambo cast down his head without reply.

"Did not my brethren know," resumed Manangani, "that there was an exchange of shots between the *Annonciation* and the custom-house officers, and that the capture of the vessel would have ruined our projects of conspiracy?"

A murmur of approbation received the words of the Indian.

"Those of my brethren who will wait before they judge will be the beloved of my heart," resumed the Sambo; "who knows whether my son Martin Paz will not one day re-appear? Listen now; the arms which have been sent us from Sechura are in our power; they are concealed in the mountains of the Cordilleras, and ready to do their office when you shall be prepared to do your duty."

"And what delays us?" said a young Indian; "we have sharpened our knives and are waiting."

"Let the hour come," said the Sambo; "do my brethren know what enemy their arms should strike first?"

Pub of the indian conspirators.

"Those mestizoes who treat us as slaves, and strike us with the hand and whip, like restive mules."

"These are the monopolizers of the riches of the soil, who will not suffer us to purchase a little comfort for our old age."

"You are mistaken; and your first blows must be struck elsewhere," said the Sambo, growing animated; "these are not the men who have dared for three hundred years past to tread the soil of our ancestors; it is not these rich men gorged with gold who have dragged to the tomb the sons of Manco-Capac; no, it is these proud Spaniards whom Fate has thrust on our independent shores! These are the true conquerors of whom you are the true slaves! If they have no longer wealth, they have authority; and, in spite of Peruvian emancipation, they crush and trample upon our natural rights. Let us forget what we are, to remember what our fathers have been!"

"*Anda! anda!*" exclaimed the assembly, with stamps of approbation.

After a few moments of silence, the Sambo assured himself, by interrogating various conspirators, that the friends of Cusco and of all Bolivia were ready to strike as a single man.

Then, resuming with fire:

"And our brethren of the mountains, brave Manangani, if they have all a heart of hatred equal to thine, a courage equal to thine, they will fall on Lima like an avalanche from the summit of the Cordilleras."

"The Sambo shall not complain of their boldness on the day appointed. Let the Indian leave the city, he shall not go far without seeing throng around him *zambos* burning for vengeance! In the gorges of San Cristoval and the Amancaës, more than one is couched on his *poncho*, with his poignard at his girdle, waiting until a long carbine shall be confided to his skillful hand. They also have not forgotten that they have to revenge on the vain Spaniards the defeat of Manco-Capac."

"Well said! Manangani; it is the god of hatred who speaks from thy mouth. My brethren shall know before long him whom their chiefs have chosen to lead this great vengeance. President Gambarra is seeking only to consolidate his power; Bolivar is afar, Santa Cruz has been driven away; we can act with certainty. In a few days, the fête of the Amancaës will summon our oppressors to pleasure; then, let each be ready to march, and let the news be carried to the most remote villages of Bolivia."

At this moment three Indians entered the great hall. The Sambo hastened to meet them.

"Well?" said he to them.

"The body of Martin Paz has not been recovered; we have sounded the river in every direction; our most skillful divers have explored it with religious care, and the son of the Sambo cannot have perished in the waters of the Rimac."

"Have they killed him? What has become of him? Oh! wo, wo to them if they have killed my son! Let my brethren separate in silence; let each return to his post, look, watch and wait!"

The Indians went out and dispersed; the Sambo alone remained with Manangani, who asked him:

"Does the Sambo know what sentiment conducted his son to San Lazaro? The Sambo, I trust, is sure of his son?"

The eyes of the Indian flashed, and the blood mounted to his cheek. The ferocious Manangani recoiled.

But the Indian controlled himself, and said:

"If Martin Paz has betrayed his brethren, I will first kill all those to whom he has given his friendship, all those to whom he has given his love! Then I will kill him, and myself afterward, that nothing may be left beneath the sun of an infamous, and dishonored race."

At this moment, the *padrona* opened the door of the room, advanced toward the Sambo, and handed him a billet directed to his address.

"Who gave you this?" said he.

"I do not know; this paper may have been designedly forgotten by a *chica*-drinker. I found it on the table."

"Have there been any but Indians here?"

"There have been none but Indians."

The *padrona* went out; the Sambo unfolded the billet, and read aloud:

"A young girl has prayed for the return of Martin Paz, for she has not forgotten that the young Indian protected her and risked his life for her. If the Sambo has any news of his poor son, or any hope of finding him, let him surround his arm with a red handkerchief; there are eyes which see him pass daily."

The Sambo crushed the billet in his hand.

"The unhappy boy," said he, "has suffered himself to be caught by the eyes of a woman."

The hostess gave him a sheet of paper.

"Who is this woman?" asked Manangani.

"It is not an Indian," replied the Sambo, observing the billet; "it is some young girl of the other classes. Martin Paz, I no longer know thee!"

"Shall you do what this woman requests?"

"No," replied the Indian, violently; "let her lose all hope of seeing him again; let her die, if she will."

And the Sambo tore the billet in a rage.

"It must have been an Indian who brought this billet," observed Manangani.

"Oh, it cannot have been one of ours! He must have known that I often came to this inn, but I will set my foot in it no more. We have occupied ourselves long enough with trifling affairs," resumed he, coldly; "let my brother return to the mountains; I will remain to watch over the city. We shall see whether the fête of the Amancaës will be joyous for the oppressors or the oppressed!"

The two Indians separated.

The plan of the conspiracy was well conceived and the hour of its execution well chosen. Peru, almost depopulated, counted only a small number of Spaniards and mestizoes. The invasion of the Indians, gathered from every direction, from the forests of Brazil, as well as the mountains of Chili and the plains of La Plata, would cover the theatre of war with a formidable army. The great cities, like Lima, Cusco, Puña, might be utterly destroyed; and it was not to be expected that the Colombian troops, so recently driven away by the Peruvian government, would come to the assistance of their enemies in peril.

This social overturn might therefore have succeeded, if the secret had remained buried in the hearts of the Indians, and there surely could not be traitors among them?

But they were ignorant that a man had obtained private audience of the President Gambarra. This man informed him that the schooner *Annonciation* had been captured from him by Indian pirates! That it had been laden with arms of all sorts; that canoes had unloaded it at the mouth of the Rimac; and he claimed a high indemnity for the service he thus rendered to the Peruvian government.

And yet this man had let his vessel to the agents of the Sambo; he had received for it a considerable sum, and had come to sell the secret which he had surprised.

By these traits the reader will recognize the Jew Samuel.

Chapter VI

THE BETROTHAL

ANDRÉ CERTA, ENTIRELY RECOVERED, sure of the death of Martin Paz, pressed his marriage: he was impatient to parade the young and beautiful Jewess through the streets of Lima.

Sarah constantly manifested toward him a haughty indifference; but he cared not for it, considering her as an article of sale, for which he had paid a hundred thousand piasters.

And yet André Certa suspected the Jew, and with good reason; if the contract was dishonorable, the contractors were still more so. So the mestizo wished to have a secret interview with Samuel, and took him one day to the Baths of Chorillos.

He was not sorry, besides, to try the chances of play before his wedding: public gaming, prohibited at Lima, is perfectly tolerated elsewhere. The passion of the Limanian ladies and gentlemen for this hazardous amusement is singular and irresistible.

The games were open some days before the arrival of the Marquis Don Vegal; thenceforth there was a perpetual movement of the populace on the road from Lima: some came on foot, who returned in carriages; others were about to risk and lose the last remnants of their fortunes.

Don Vegal and Martin Paz took no part in these exciting pleasures. The reveries of the young Indian had more noble causes; he was thinking of Sarah and of his benefactor.

The concourse of the Limanians to the Baths of Chorillos was without danger for him; little known by the inhabitants of the city, like all the mountain Indians he easily concealed himself from all eyes.

After his evening walk with the marquis, Martin Paz would return to his room, and leaning his elbow on the window, pass long hours in allowing his tumultuous thoughts to wander over the Pacific Ocean. Don Vegal lodged in a neighboring chamber, and guarded him with paternal tenderness.

The Spaniard always remembered the daughter of Samuel, whom he had so unexpectedly seen at prayer in the Catholic temple. But he had not dared to confide this important secret to Martin Paz while instructing him by degrees in Christian truths; he feared to re-animate sentiments which he wished to extinguish—for the poor Indian, unknown and proscribed, must renounce all hope of happiness! Father Joachim kept Don Vegal informed of the progress of affairs: the police had at last ceased to trouble themselves about Martin Paz; and with time and the influence of his protector, the Indian, become a man of merit and capable of great things, might one day take rank in the highest Peruvian society.

Weary of the uncertainty into which his incognito plunged him, Paz resolved to know what had become of the young Jewess. Thanks to his Spanish costume, he could glide into a gaming-saloon, and listen to the conversation of its various frequenters. André Certa was a man of so much importance, that his marriage, if it was approaching, would be the subject of conversation.

One evening, instead of directing his steps toward the sea, the Indian climbed over the high rocks on which the principal habitations of Chorillos are built; a house, fronted by broad stone steps, struck his eyes—he entered it without noise.

The day had been hard for many of the wealthy Limanians; some among them, exhausted with the fatigues of the preceding night, were reposing on the ground, wrapped in their *ponchos.*

Other players were seated before a large green table, divided into four compartments by two lines, which intersected each other at the centre in right angles; on each of these compartments were the first letters of the words *azar* and *suerte,* (chance and fate,) A and S.

At this moment, the parties of the *monte* were animated; a mestizo was pursuing the unfavorable chance with feverish ardor.

"Two thousand piasters!" exclaimed he.

The banker shook the dice, and the player burst into imprecations.

"Four thousand piasters!" said he, again. And he lost once more.

Martin Paz, protected by the obscurity of the saloon, could look the player in the face, and he turned pale.

It was André Certa!

Near him, was standing the Jew Samuel.

"You have played enough, Señor André," said Samuel to him; "the luck is not for you."

"What business is it of yours?" replied the mestizo, roughly.

Samuel bent down to his ear.

"If it is not my business, it is your business to break off these habits during the days which precede your marriage."

"Eight thousand piasters!" resumed André Certa.

He lost again: the mestizo suppressed a curse and the banker resumed—"Play on!"

André Certa, drawing from his pocket some bills, was about to have hazarded a considerable sum; he had even deposited it on one of the tables, and the banker, shaking his dice, was about to have decided its fate, when a sign from Samuel stopped him short. The Jew bent again to the ear of the mestizo, and said—

View of the bathing area of Chorillos.

"If nothing remains to you to conclude our bargain, it shall be broken off this evening!"

André Certa shrugged his shoulders, took up his money, and went out.

"Continue now," said Samuel to the banker; "you may ruin this gentleman after his marriage."

The banker bowed submissively. The Jew Samuel was the founder and proprietor of the games of Chorillos. Wherever there was a *real* to be made this man was to be met with.

He followed the mestizo; and finding him on the stone steps, said to him—

"I have secrets of importance to communicate. Where can we converse in safety?"

"Wherever you please," replied Certa, roughly.

"Señor, let not your passions ruin your prospects. I would neither confide my secret to the most carefully closed chambers, nor the most lonely plains. If you pay me dearly for it, it is because it is worth telling and worth keeping."

As they spoke thus, these two men had reached the sea, near the cabins destined for the use of the bathers. They knew not that they were seen, heard and watched by Martin Paz, who glided like a serpent in the shadow.

"Let us take a canoe," said André, "and go out into the open sea; the sharks may, perhaps, show themselves discreet."

André detached from the shore a little boat, and threw some money to its guardian. Samuel embarked with him, and the mestizo pushed off. He vigorously plied two flexible oars, which soon took them a mile from the shore.

But as he saw the canoe put off, Martin Paz, concealed in a crevice of the rock, hastily undressed, and precipitating himself into the sea, swam vigorously toward the boat.

The sun had just buried his last rays in the waves of the ocean, and darkness hovered over the crests of the waves.

Martin Paz had not once reflected that sharks of the most dangerous species frequented these fatal shores. He stopped not far from the boat of the mestizo, and listened.

"*But what proof of the identity of the daughter shall I carry to the father?*" asked André Certa of the Jew.

"You will recall to him the circumstances under which he lost her."

"What were these circumstances?"

Martin Paz, now scarcely above the waves, listened without understanding. In a girdle attached to his body, he had a poignard; he waited.

"Her father," said the Jew, "lived at Concencion, in Chili: he was then the great nobleman he is now; only his fortune equalled his nobility. Obliged to come to Lima on business, he set out alone, leaving at Concencion his wife, and child aged fifteen months. The climate of Peru agreed with him, and he sent for the marchioness to rejoin him. She embarked on the *San-José* of Valparaiso, with her confidential servants.

"I was going to Peru in the same ship. The *San-José* was about to enter the harbor of Lima; but, near Juan Fernandez, was struck by a terrific hurricane, which disabled her and threw her on her side—it was the affair of half an hour. The *San-José* filled with water and was slowly sinking; the passengers and crew took refuge in the boat, but at sight of the furious waves, the marchioness refused to enter it; she pressed her infant in her arms, and remained in the ship. I remained with her—the boat was swallowed up at a hundred fathoms from the *San-José*, with all her crew. We were alone—the tempest blew with increasing violence. As my fortune was not on board, I had nothing to lose. The *San-José*, having five feet of water in her hold, drifted on the rocks of the shore, where she broke to pieces. The young woman was thrown into the sea with her daughter: fortunately, for me," said the Jew, with a gloomy smile, "I could seize the child, and reach the shore with it."

"All these details are exact?"

"Perfectly so. The father will recognize them. I had done a good day's work, señor; since she is worth to me the hundred thousand piasters which you are about to pay me. Now, let the marriage take place to-morrow."

"What does this mean?" asked Martin Paz of himself, still swimming in the shadow.

"Here is my pocket-book, with the hundred thousand piasters—take it, Master Samuel," replied André Certa to the Jew.

"Thanks, Señor André," said the Israelite, seizing the treasure; "take this receipt in exchange—I pledge myself to restore you double this sum, if you do not become a member of one of the proudest families of Spain."

"You played enough," Samuel said.

But the Indian had not heard this last sentence; he had dived to avoid the approach of the boat, and his eyes could see a shapeless mass gliding rapidly toward him. He thought it was the canoe—he was mistaken.

It was a *tintorea*; a shark of the most ferocious species.

Martin Paz did not quail, or he would have been lost. The animal approached him—the Indian dived; but he was obliged to come up, in order to breathe… He looked at the sky, as if he was never to behold it again. The stars sparkled above his head; the *tintorea* continued to approach. A vigorous blow with his tail struck the swimmer; Martin Paz felt his slimy scales brush his breast. The shark, in order to snatch at him, turned on his back and opened his jaws, armed with a triple row of teeth. Martin Paz saw the white belly of the animal gleam beneath the wave, and with a rapid hand struck it with his poignard.

Suddenly he found the waters around him red with blood. He dived—came up again at ten fathoms' distance—thought of the daughter of Samuel; and seeing nothing more of the boat of the mestizo, regained the shore in a few strokes, already forgetting that he had just escaped death.

He quickly rejoined Don Vegal. The latter, not having found him on his return, was anxiously awaiting him. Paz made no allusion to his recent adventures; but seemed to take a lively pleasure in his conversation.

But the next day Martin Paz had left Chorillos, and Don Vegal, tortured with anxiety, hastily returned to Lima.

The marriage of André Certa with the daughter of the wealthy Samuel, was an important event. The beautiful señoras had not given themselves a moment's rest; they had exhausted their ingenuity to invent some pretty corsage or novel head-dress; they had wearied themselves in trying without cessation the most varied toilets.

Numerous preparations were also going on in the house of Samuel; it was a part of the Jew's plan to give great publicity to the marriage of Sarah. The frescoes which adorned his dwelling according to the Spanish custom, had been newly painted; the richest hangings fell in large folds at the windows and doors of the habitation. Furniture carved in the latest fashion, of precious or fragrant wood, was crowded in vast saloons, impregnated with a delicious coolness. Rare shrubs, the productions of warm countries, seized the eye with their splendid colors, and one would have thought Spring had stolen along the balconies and terraces, to inundate them with flowers and perfumes.

Meanwhile, amid these smiling marvels, the young girl was weeping; Sarah no longer had hope, since the Sambo had none; and the Sambo had no hope, since he wore no sign of hope! The negro Liberta had watched the steps of the old Indian; he had seen nothing. Ah! if the poor child could have followed the impulses of her heart, she would have immured herself in one of those tranquil *beaterios*, to die there amid tears and prayer.

Urged by an irresistible attraction to the doctrines of Catholicism, the young Jewess had been secretly converted; by the cares of the good Father Joachim, she had been won over to a religion more in accordance with her feelings than that in which she had been educated. If

Samuel had destined her for a Jew, she would have avowed her faith; but, about to espouse a Catholic, she reserved for her husband the secret of her conversion.

Father Joachim, in order to avoid scandal, and besides, better read in his breviary than in the human heart, had suffered Sarah to believe in the death of Martin Paz. The conversion of the young girl was the most important thing to him; he saw it assured by her union with André Certa, and he sought to accustom her to the idea of this marriage, the conditions of which he was far from respecting.

At last the day so joyous for some, so sad for others, had arrived. André Certa had invited the entire city to his nuptials; his invitations were refused by the noble families, who excused themselves on various pretexts. The mestizo, meanwhile, proudly held up his head, and scarcely looked at those of his own class. The little Milleflores in vain essayed his humblest vows; but he consoled himself with the idea that he was about to figure as an active party in the repast which was to follow.

In the meantime, the young mestizoes were discoursing with him in the brilliant saloons of the Jew, and the crowd of guests thronged around André Certa, who proudly displayed the splendors of his toilet.

The contract was soon to be signed; the sun had long been set, and the young girl had not appeared.

Doubtless she was discussing with her duenna and her maids the place of a ribbon or the choice of an ornament. Perhaps, that enchanting timidity which so beautifully adorns the cheeks of a young girl, detained her still from their inquisitive regards.

The Jew Samuel seemed a prey to secret uneasiness; André Certa bent his brow in an impatient manner; a sort of embarrassment was depicted on the countenance of more than one guest, while the thousand of wax-lights, reflected by the mirrors, filled the saloon with dazzling splendor.

Without, a man was wandering in mortal anxiety; it was the Marquis Don Vegal.

Chapter VII

ALL INTERESTS AT STAKE

MEANWHILE, SARAH WAS LEFT ALONE, alone with her anguish and her grief! She was about to give up her whole life to a man whom she did not love! She leaned over the perfumed balcony of her chamber, which overlooked the interior gardens. Through the green jalousies, her ear listened to the sounds of the slumbering country. Her lace mantle, gliding over her arms, revealed a profusion of diamonds sparkling on her shoulders. Her sorrow, proud and majestic, appeared through all her ornaments, and she might have been taken for one of those beautiful Greek slaves, nobly draped in their antique garments.

Suddenly her glance rested on a man who was gliding silently among the avenues of the magnolia; she recognized him; it was Liberta, her servant. He seemed to be watching some invisible enemy, now sheltering himself behind a statue, now crouching on the ground.

Sarah was afraid, and looked around her. She was alone, entirely alone. Her eyes rested on the gardens, and she became pale, paler still! Before her was transpiring a terrible scene. Liberta was in the grasp of a man of tall stature, who had thrown him down; stifled sighs proved that a robust hand was pressing the lips of the Indian.

The young girl, summoning all her courage, was about to cry out, when she saw the two men rise! The negro was looking fixedly at his adversary.

"It is you, then! it is you!" exclaimed he.

And he followed this man in a strange stupefaction. They arrived beneath the balcony of Sarah. Suddenly, before she had time to utter a cry, Martin Paz appeared to her, like a phantom from another world;

and, like the negro when overthrown by the Indian, the young girl, bending before the glance of Martin Paz, could in her turn only repeat these words,

"It is you, then! it is you!"

The young Indian fixed on her his motionless eyes, and said:

"Does the betrothed hear the sound of the festival? The guests are thronging into the saloons to see happiness radiate from her countenance! Is it then a victim, prepared for the sacrifice, who is about to present herself to their impatient eyes? Is it with these features, pale with sorrow, with eyes in which sparkle bitter tears, that the young girl is to appear herself before her betrothed?"

Martin Paz spoke thus, in a tone full of sympathizing sadness, and Sarah listened vaguely as to those harmonies which we hear in dreams!

The young Indian resumed with infinite sweetness:

"Since the soul of the young girl is in mourning, let her look beyond the house of her father, beyond the city where she suffers and weeps; beyond the mountains, the palm-trees lift up their heads in freedom, the birds strike the air with an independent wing; men have immensity to live in, and the young girls may unfold their spirits and their hearts!"

Sarah raised her head toward Martin Paz. The Indian had drawn himself up to his full height, and with his arm extended toward the summits of the Cordilleras, was pointing out to the young girl the path to liberty.

Sarah felt herself constrained by an irresistible force. Already the sound of voices reached her; they approached her chamber; her father was undoubtedly about to enter; perhaps her lover would accompany him! The Indian suddenly extinguished the lamp suspended above his head. A whistling, similar to the cry of the *cilguero*, and reminding one of that heard on the Plaza-Mayor, pierced the silent darkness of night; the young girl swooned.

The door opened hastily; Samuel and André Certa entered. The darkness was profound; some servants ran with torches. The chamber was empty.

"Death and fury!" exclaimed the mestizo.

"Where is she?" asked Samuel.

"You are responsible for her," said André, brutally.

At these words, the Jew felt a cold sweat freeze even his bones.

"Help! help!" he exclaimed.

And, followed by his domestics, he sprang out of the house.

Martin Paz fled rapidly through the streets of the city. The negro Liberta followed him; but did not appear disposed to dispute with him the possession of the young girl.

At two hundred paces from the dwelling of the Jew, Paz found some Indians of his companions, who had assembled at the whistle uttered by him.

"To our mountain *ranchos*!" exclaimed he.

"To the house of the Marquis Don Vegal!" said another voice behind him.

Martin Paz turned; the Spaniard was at his side.

"Will you not confide this young girl to me?" asked the marquis.

The Indian bent his head, and said in a low voice to his companions:

"To the dwelling of the Marquis Don Vegal!"

They turned their steps in this direction.

An extreme confusion reigned then in the saloons of the Jew. The news of Sarah's disappearance was a thunderbolt; the friends of André hastened to follow him. The *faubourg* of San Lazaro was explored, hastily searched; but nothing could be discovered. Samuel tore his hair in despair. During the whole night the most active research was useless.

"Martin Paz is living!" exclaimed André Certa, in a moment of fury.

And the presentiment quickly acquired confirmation. The police were immediately informed of the elopement; its most active agents bestirred themselves; the Indians were closely watched, and if the retreat of the young girl was not discovered, evident proofs of an approaching revolt came to light, which accorded with the denunciations of the Jew.

André Certa lavished gold freely, but could learn nothing. Meanwhile, the gate-keepers declared that they had seen no person leave Lima; the young girl must therefore be concealed in the city.

Liberta, who returned to his master, was often interrogated; but no person seemed more astonished than himself at the elopement of Sarah.

Meanwhile, one man besides André Certa had seen in the disappearance of the young Jewess, a proof of the existence of Martin Paz;

Dance of Lima (the Samacuera) to the sound of guitars and pumpkin drums.

it was the Sambo. He was wandering in the streets of Lima, when the cry uttered by the Indian fixed his attention; it was a signal of rally well known to him! The Sambo was therefore a spectator of the capture of the young girl, and followed her to the dwelling of the marquis.

The Spaniard entered by a secret door, of which he alone had the key; so that his domestics suspected nothing. Martin Paz carried the young girl in his arms and laid her on a bed.

When Don Vegal, who had returned to re-enter by the principal door, reached the chamber where Sarah was reposing, he found Martin Paz kneeling beside her. The marquis was about to reproach the Indian with his conduct, when the latter said to him:

"You see, my father, whether I love you! Ah! why did you throw yourself in my way? We should have been already free in our mountains. But how, should I not have obeyed your words?"

Don Vegal knew not what to reply, his heart was seized with a powerful emotion. He felt how much he was beloved by Martin Paz.

"The day on which Sarah shall quit your dwelling to be restored to her father and her betrothed," sighed the Indian, "you will have a son and a friend less in the world."

As he said these last words, Paz moistened with his tears the hand of Don Vegal. They were the first tears this man had shed!

The reproaches of Don Vegal died away before this respectful submission. The young girl had become his guest; she was sacred! He could not help admiring Sarah, still in a swoon; he was prepared to love her, of whose conversion he had been a witness, and whom he would have been pleased to bestow as a companion upon the young Indian.

It was then that, on opening her eyes, Sarah found herself in the presence of a stranger.

"Where am I?" said she, with a sentiment of terror.

"With a generous man who has permitted me to call him my father," replied Martin Paz, pointing to the Spaniard.

The young girl, restored by the voice of the Indian to a consciousness of her position, covered her face with her trembling hands, and began to sob.

"Withdraw, friend," said Don Vegal to the young man; "withdraw."

Martin Paz slowly left the room, not without having pressed the hand of the Spaniard, and cast on Sarah a lingering look.

Then Don Vegal bestowed upon this poor child consolations of exquisite delicacy; he conveyed in suitable language his sentiments of nobility and honor. Attentive and resigned, the young girl comprehended what danger she had escaped; and she confided her future happiness to the care of the Spaniard. But amid phrases interrupted by sighs and mingled with tears, Don Vegal perceived the intense attachment of this simple heart for him whom she called her deliverer. He induced Sarah to take some repose, and watched over her with the solicitude of a father.

Martin Paz comprehended the duties that honor required of him, and, in spite of perils and dangers, would not pass the night beneath the roof of Don Vegal.

He therefore went out; his head was burning, his blood was boiling with fever in his veins.

He had not gone a hundred paces in the street, when five or six men threw themselves upon him, and, notwithstanding his obstinate defense, succeeded in binding him. Martin Paz uttered a cry of despair, which was lost in the night. He believed himself in the power of his enemies, and gave a last thought to the young girl.

A short time afterward the Indian was deposited in a room. The bandage which had covered his eyes was taken off. He looked around him, and saw himself in the lower hall of that tavern where his brethren had organized their approaching revolt.

The Sambo, Manangani, and others, surrounded him. A gleam of indignation flashed from his eyes, which was reciprocated by his captors.

"My son had then no pity on my tears," said the Sambo, "since he suffered me for so long a time to believe in his death?"

"Is it on the eve before a revolt that Martin Paz, our chief, should be found in the camp of our enemies?"

Martin Paz replied neither to his father, nor to Manangani.

"So our most important interests have been sacrificed to a woman!"

As he spoke thus, Manangani had approached Martin Paz; a poignard was gleaming in his hand. Martin Paz did not even look at him.

"Let us first speak," said the Sambo; "we will act afterward. If my son fails to conduct his brethren to the combat, I shall know now on whom to avenge his treason. Let him take care! the daughter of the Jew Samuel is not so well concealed that she can escape our hatred. My son will reflect. Struck with a mortal condemnation, proscribed, wandering among our masters, he will not have a stone on which to rest his sorrows. If, on the contrary, we resume our ancient country and our ancient power, Martin Paz, the chief of numerous tribes, may bestow upon his betrothed both happiness and glory."

Martin Paz remained silent; but a terrific conflict was going on within him. The Sambo had roused the most sensitive chords of his proud nature to vibrate; placed between a life of fatigues, of dangers, of despair, and an existence happy, honored, illustrious, he could not hesitate. But should he then abandon the Marquis Don Vegal, whose noble hopes destined him as the deliverer of Peru!

"Oh!" thought he, as he looked at his father, "they will kill Sarah, if I forsake them."

"What does my son reply to us?" imperiously demanded the Sambo.

"That Martin Paz is indispensable to your projects; that he enjoys a supreme authority over the Indians of the city; that he leads them at his will, and, at a sign, could have them dragged to death. He must therefore resume his place in the revolt, in order to ensure victory."

The bonds which still enchained him were detached by order of the Sambo; Martin Paz arose free among his brethren.

"My son," said the Indian, who was observing him attentively, "to-morrow, during the fête of the Amancaës, our brethren will fall like an avalanche on the unarmed Limanians. There is the road to the Cordilleras, there is the road to the city; you will go wherever your good pleasure shall lead you. To-morrow! to-morrow! you will find more than one mestizo breast to break your poignard against. You are free."

"To the mountains!" exclaimed Martin Paz, with a stern voice.

The Indian had again become an Indian amid the hatred which surrounded him.

"To the mountains," repeated he, "and wo to our enemies, wo!"

Sarah at the church of Santa Anna.

And the rising sun illumined with its earliest rays the council of the Indian chiefs in the heart of the Cordilleras.

These rays were joyless to the heart of the poor young girl, who wept and prayed. The marquis had summoned Father Joachim; and the worthy man had there met his beloved penitent. What happiness was it for her to kneel at the feet of the old priest, and to pour out her anguish and her afflictions.

But Sarah could not longer remain in the dwelling of the Spaniard. Father Joachim suggested this to Don Vegal, who knew not what part to take, for he was a prey to extreme anxiety. What had become of Martin Paz? He had fled the house. Was he in the power of his enemies? Oh! how the Spaniard regretted having suffered him to leave

The festival of the Amancaés in Lima.

it during that night of alarms! He sought him with the ardor, with the affection of a father; he found him not.

"My old friend," said he to Joachim, "the young girl is in safety near you; do not leave her during this fatal night."

"But her father, who seeks her—her betrothed, who awaits her?"

"One day—one single day! You know not whose existence is bound to that of this child. One day—one single day! at least until I find Martin Paz, he whom my heart and God have named my son!"

Father Joachim returned to the young girl; Don Vegal went out and traversed the streets of Lima.

The Spaniard was surprised at the noise, the commotion, the agitation of the city. It was that the great fête of the Amancaës, forgotten by him alone, the 24th of June, the day of St. John, had arrived. The neighboring mountains were covered with verdure and flowers; the inhabitants, on foot, on horseback, in carriages, were repairing to a celebrated table-land, situated at half a league from Lima, where the spectators enjoyed an admirable prospect; mestizoes and Indians mingled in the common fête; they walked gayly by groups of relatives or friends; each group, calling itself by the name of *partida*, carried its provisions, and was preceded by a player on the guitar, who chanted, accompanying himself, the most popular *yaravis* and *llantos*. These joyous promenaders advanced with cries, sports, endless jests, through the fields of maize and of *alfalfa*, through the groves of banana, whose fruits hung to the ground; they traversed those beautiful *alamedas*, planted with willows, and forests of citron, and orange-trees, whose intoxicating perfumes were mingled with the wild fragrance from the mountains. All along the road, traveling cabarets offered to the promenaders the brandy of *pisco* and the *chica*, whose copious libations excited to laughter and clamor; cavaliers made their horses caracole in the midst of the throng, and rivaled each other in swiftness, address, and dexterity; all the dances in vogue, from the *loudon* to the *mismis*, from the *boleros* to the *zamacuecas*, agitated and hurried on the *caballeros* and black-eyed *sambas*. The sounds of the *viguela* were soon no longer sufficient for the disordered movements of the dancers; the musicians uttered wild cries, which stimulated them to delirium; the spectators beat the measure with their feet and hands, and the exhausted couples sunk one after another to the ground.

There reigned in this fête, which derives its name from the little mountain-flowers, an inconceivable transport and freedom; and yet no private brawl mingled among the cries of public rejoicing; a few lancers on horseback, ornamented with their shining cuirasses, maintained here and there order among the populace.

The various classes of Limanian society mingled in these rejoicings, which are repeated every day throughout the month of July. Pretty *tapadas* laughingly elbow beautiful girls, who bravely come, with uncovered faces, to meet joyous cavaliers; and when at last this multitude arrive at the *plateau* of the Amancaës, an immense clamor of admiration is repeated by the mountain echoes.

At the feet of the spectators extends the ancient city of kings, proudly lifting toward heaven its towers and its steeples, whose bells are ringing joyous peals. San Pedro, Saint Augustine, the Cathedral, attract the eye to their roofs, resplendent with the rays of the sun. San Domingo, the rich church, the Madonna of which is never clad in the same garments two days in succession, raises above her neighbors her tapering spire; on the right, the vast plains of the Pacific Ocean are undulating to the breath of the occidental breeze, and the eye, as it roves from Callao to Lima, rests on those funereal *chulpas*, the last remains of the great dynasty of the Incas; at the horizon, Cape Morro-Solar frames, with its sloping hills, the wonderful splendors of this picture.

So the Limanians are never satisfied with these admirable prospects, and their noisy approbation deafens every year the echoes of San Cristoval and the Amancaës.

Now, while they fearlessly enjoyed these picturesque views, and were giving themselves up to an irresistible delight, a gloomy bloody funereal drama was preparing on the snowy summits of the Cordilleras.

Chapter VIII

CONQUERORS AND CONQUERED

A PREY TO HIS BLIND GRIEF, Don Vegal walked at random. After having lost his daughter, the hope of his race and of his love, was he about to see himself also deprived of the child of his adoption whom he had wrested from death? Don Vegal had forgotten Sarah, to think only of Martin Paz.

He was struck with the great number of Indians, of *zambos*, of *chiños*, who were wandering about the streets; these men, who usually took an active part in the sports of the Amancaës, were now walking silently with singular pre-occupation. Often some busy chief gave them a secret order, and went on his way; and all, notwithstanding their *detours*, were assembling by degrees in the wealthiest quarters of Lima, in proportion as the Limanians were scattered abroad in the country.

Don Vegal, absorbed in his own researches, soon forgot this singular state of things. He traversed San Lazaro throughout, saw André Certa there, enraged and armed, and the Jew Samuel, in the extremity of distress, not for the loss of his daughter, but for the loss of his hundred thousand piasters; but he found not Martin Paz, whom he was impatiently seeking. He ran to the consistorial prison. Nothing! He returned home. Nothing! He mounted his horse and hastened to Chorillos. Nothing! He returned at last, exhausted with fatigue, to Lima; the clock of the cathedral was striking four.

Don Vegal remarked some groups of Indians before his dwelling; but he could not, without compromising the man of whom he was in search, ask them—

"Where is Martin Paz?"

He re-entered, more despairing than ever.

Immediately a man emerged from a neighboring alley, and came directly to the Indians. This man was the Sambo.

"The Spaniard has returned," said he to them; "you know him now; he is one of the representatives of the race which crushes us—wo to him!"

"And when shall we strike?"

"When five o'clock sounds, and the tocsin from the mountain gives the signal of vengeance."

Then the Sambo marched with hasty steps to the *chingana*, and rejoined the chief of the revolt.

Meanwhile the sun had begun to sink beneath the horizon; it was the hour in which the Limanian aristocracy went in its turn to the Amancaës; the richest toilets shone in the equipages which defiled to the right and left beneath the trees along the road; there was an inextricable mêlée of foot-passengers, carriages, horses; a confusion of cries, songs, instruments, and vociferations.

The clock on the tower of the cathedral suddenly struck five! and a shrill funereal sound vibrated through the air; the tocsin thundered over the crowd, frozen in its delirium.

An immense cry resounded in the city. From every square, every street, every house issued the Indians, with arms in their hands, and fury in their eyes. The principal places of the city were thronged with these men, some of whom shook above their heads burning torches!

"Death to the Spaniards! death to the oppressors!" such was the watch-word of the rebels.

Those who attempted to return to Lima must have recoiled before these masses; but the summits of the hills were quickly covered with other enemies, and all retreat was impossible; the *zambos* precipitated themselves like a thunderbolt on this crowd, exhausted with the fatigues of the festival, while the mountain Indians cleared for themselves a bloody path to rejoin their brethren of the city.

Imagine the aspect presented by Lima at this terrible moment. The rebels had left the square of the tavern, and were scattered in all quarters; at the head of one of the columns, Martin Paz was waving the black flag—the flag of independence; while the Indians in the other streets were attacking the houses appointed to ruin, Martin Paz took possession of the Plaza-Mayor with his company; near him, Manangani was uttering ferocious yells, and proudly displaying his bloody arms.

But the soldiers of the government, forewarned of the revolt, were ranged in battle array before the palace of the president; a frightful *fusillade* greeted the insurgents at their entrance on the square; surprised by this unexpected discharge, which extended a goodly number of them on the ground, they sprang upon the troops with insurmountable impatience; a horrible mêlée followed, in which men fought body to body. Martin Paz and Manangani performed prodigies of valor, and escaped death only by miracle.

"As the girl was swimming in her tears."

It was necessary at all hazards that the palace should be taken and occupied by their men.

"Forward!" cried Martin Paz, and his voice led the Indians to the assault. Although they were crushed in every direction, they succeeded in making the body of troops around the palace recoil. Already had Manangani sprang on the first steps; but he suddenly stopped as the opening ranks of soldiers unmasked two pieces of cannon ready to fire on the assailants.

There was not a moment to lose; the battery must be seized before it could be discharged.

"On!" cried Manangani, addressing himself to Martin Paz.

But the young Indian had just stooped and no longer heard him, for an Indian had whispered these words in his ear:

"They are pillaging the house of Don Vegal, perhaps assassinating him!"

At these words Martin Paz recoiled. Manangani seized him by the arm; but, repulsing him with a vigorous hand, the Indian darted toward the square.

"Traitor! infamous traitor!" exclaimed Manangani, discharging his pistols at Martin Paz.

At this moment the cannons were fired, and the grape swept the Indians on the steps.

"This way, brethren," cried Martin Paz, and a few fugitives, his devoted companions, joined him; with this little company he could make his way through the soldiers.

This flight had all the consequences of treason; the Indians believed themselves abandoned by their chief. Manangani in vain attempted to bring them back to the combat; a rapid *fusillade* sent among them a shower of balls; thenceforth it was no longer possible to rally them; the confusion was at its height and the rout complete. The flames which arose in certain quarters attracted some fugitives to pillage; but the conquering soldiers pursued them with the sword, and killed a great number without mercy.

Meanwhile, Martin Paz had gained the house of Don Vegal; it was the theatre of a bloody struggle, headed by the Sambo himself; he had a double interest in being there; while contending with the Spanish noblemen, he wished to seize Sarah, as a pledge of the fidelity of his son.

On seeing Martin Paz return, he no longer doubted his treason, and turned his brethren against him.

The overthrown gate and walls of the court revealed Don Vegal, sword in hand, surrounded by his faithful servants, and contending with an invading mass. This man's courage and pride were sublime; he was the first to present himself to mortal blows, and his formidable arm had surrounded him with corpses.

But what could be done against this crowd of Indians, which was then increasing with all the conquered of the Plaza-Mayor. Don Vegal felt that his defenders were becoming exhausted, and nothing remained for him but death, when Martin Paz arrived, rapid as the thunderbolt, charged the aggressors from behind, forced them to turn against him, and, amid balls, poignard-strokes and maledictions, reached Don Vegal, to whom he made a rampart of his body. Courage revived in the hearts of the besieged.

"Well done, my son, well done!" said Don Vegal to Martin Paz, pressing his hand.

But the young Indian was gloomy.

"Well done! Martin Paz," exclaimed another voice which went to his very soul; he recognized Sarah, and his arm traced a bloody circle around him.

The company of Sambo gave way in its turn. Twenty times had this modern Brutus directed his blows against his son, without being able to reach him, and twenty times Martin had turned away the weapon about to strike his father.

Suddenly the ferocious Manangani, covered with blood, appeared beside the Sambo.

"Thou hast sworn," said he, "to avenge the treason of a wretch on his kindred, on his friends, on himself. Well, it is time! the soldiers are coming; the mestizo, André Certa, is with them."

"Come then," said the Sambo, with a ferocious laugh: "come then, for our vengeance approaches."

And both abandoned the house of Don Vegal, while their companions were being killed there. They went directly to the company who were arriving. The latter aimed at them; but without being intimidated, the Sambo approached the mestizo.

"You are André Certa," said he; "well, your betrothed is in the house of Don Vegal, and Martin Paz is about to carry her to the mountains."

Manangani stepped closer, saying "If my son is disloyal to his brethren,
I shall know how to exact a proper vengeance."

This said, the Indians disappeared. Thus the Sambo had put face to face two mortal enemies, and, deceived by the presence of Martin Paz in the house of Don Vegal, the soldiers rushed upon the dwelling of the marquis.

André Certa was intoxicated with rage. As soon as he perceived Martin Paz, he rushed upon him.

"Here!" exclaimed the young Indian, and quitting the stone steps which he had so valiantly defended, he joined the mestizo. Meanwhile the companions of Martin Paz were repulsing the soldiers body to body.

Martin Paz had seized André Certa with his powerful hand, and clasped him so closely that the mestizo could not use his pistols. They were there, foot against foot, breast against breast, their faces touched, and their glances mingled in a single gleam; their movements became rapid, even invisible; neither friends nor enemies could approach them; in this terrible embrace respiration failed, both fell. André Certa raised himself above Martin Paz, whose poignard had escaped his grasp. The mestizo raised his arm, but the Indian succeeded in seizing it before it had struck. The moment was horrible. André Certa in vain attempted to disengage himself; Martin Paz, with supernatural strength, turned against the mestizo the poignard and the arm which held it, and plunged it into his heart.

Martin Paz arose all bloody. The place was free, the soldiers flying in every direction. Martin Paz might have conquered had he remained on the Plaza-Mayor. He fell into the arms of Don Vegal.

"To the mountains, my son; flee to the mountains! now I command it."

"Is my enemy indeed dead?" said Martin Paz, returning to the corpse of André Certa.

A man was that moment searching it, and held a pocket-book which he had taken from it. Martin Paz sprang on this man and overthrew him; it was the Jew Samuel.

The Indian picked up the pocket-book, opened it hastily, searched it, uttered a cry of joy, and springing toward the marquis, put in his hand a paper on which were written these words:

"Received of the Señor André Certa the sum of 100,000 piasters; I pledge myself to restore this sum doubled, if Sarah, whom I saved from the shipwreck of the *San-José*, and whom he is about to espouse, is not the daughter and only heir of the Marquis Don Vegal.

"SAMUEL."

"My daughter! my daughter!" exclaimed the Spaniard, and he fell into the arms of Martin Paz, who carried him to the chamber of Sarah.

Alas! the young girl was no longer there; Father Joachim, bathed in his own blood, could articulate only these words:

"The Sambo!—carried off!—toward the river of Madeira!—"

And he fainted.

Chapter IX

THE CATARACTS OF THE MADEIRA

"ON! ON!" Martin Paz had exclaimed. And without saying a word, Don Vegal followed the Indian. His daughter!—he must find again his daughter! Mules were brought, prepared for a long journey among the Cordilleras; the two men mounted them, wrapped in their *ponchos*; large gaiters were attached by thongs above their knees; immense stirrups, armed with long spurs, surrounded their feet, and broad-brimmed Guayaquil hats sheltered their heads. Arms filled the holsters of each saddle; a carbine, formidable in the hands of Don Vegal, was suspended at his side. Martin Paz had encircled himself with his lasso, one extremity of which was fixed to the harness of his mule.

The Spaniard and the Indian spurred their horses to their utmost speed. At the moment of leaving the walls of the city they were joined by an Indian equipped like themselves. It was Liberta—Don Vegal recognized him; the faithful servant wished to share in their pursuit.

Martin Paz knew all the plains, all the mountains, which they were to traverse; he knew among what savage tribes, into what desert country the Sambo had conveyed his betrothed. His betrothed! he no longer dared give this name to the daughter of Don Vegal.

"My son," said the latter, "have you any hope in your heart?"

"As much as hatred and tenderness."

"The daughter of the Jew, in becoming my blood, has not ceased to be thine."

"Let us press on!" hastily replied Martin Paz.

On their way the travelers saw a great number of Indians flying to regain their *ranchos* amid the mountains. The defection of Martin

Paz had been followed by defeat. If the *émeute* had triumphed in some places, it had received its death-blow at Lima.

The three cavaliers traveled rapidly, having but one idea, one object. They soon buried themselves among the almost impracticable passes of the Cordilleras. Difficult pathways circulated through these reddish masses, planted here and there with cocoanut and pine trees; the cedars, cotton-trees, and aloes were left behind them, with the plains covered with maize and lucerne; some thorny cactuses sometimes pricked their mules, and made them hesitate on the verge of precipices.

It was a difficult task to traverse the Cordilleras during these summer months; the melting of snows beneath the sun of June often made unforeseen cataracts spout from beneath the steps of the traveler; often frightful masses, detaching themselves from the summits of the peaks, were engulfed near them in fathomless abysses!

But they continued their march, fearing neither the hurricane nor the cold of these high solitudes; they traveled day and night, finding neither cities nor dwellings where they might for a moment repose; happy if in some deserted hut they found a mat of *tortora* upon which to extend their wearied limbs, some pieces of meat dried in the sun, some calabashes full of muddy water.

They reached at last the summit of the Andes, 14,000 feet above the level of the sea. There, no more trees, no more vegetation; sometimes an *oso* or *ucuman*, a sort of enormous black bear, came to meet them. Often, during the afternoon, they were enveloped in those formidable storms of the Cordilleras, which raise whirlwinds of snow from the loftiest summits. Don Vegal sometimes paused, unaccustomed to these frightful perils. Martin Paz then supported him in his arms, and sheltered him against the drifting snow. And yet lightnings flashed from the clouds, and thunders broke over these barren peaks, and filled the mountain recesses with their terrific roar.

At this point, the most elevated of the Andes, the travelers were seized with a malady called by the Indians *soroche*, which deprives the most intrepid man of his courage and his strength. A superhuman will is then necessary to keep one from falling motionless on the stones of the road, and being devoured by those immense condors which display above their vast wings! These three men spoke little; each wrapped himself in the silence which these vast deserts inspired.

On the eastern slope of the Cordilleras, they hoped to find traces of their enemies; they therefore traveled on, and were at last descending the chain of mountains; but the Andes are composed of a great number of salient peaks, so that inaccessible precipices were constantly rising before them.

Nevertheless they soon found the trees of inferior levels; the llamas, the vigonias, which feed on the thin grass, announced the neighborhood of men. Sometimes they met *gauchos* conducting their *arias* of mules; and more than one *capataz* (leader of a convoy) exchanged fresh animals for their exhausted ones.

In this manner they reached the immense virgin forests which cover the plains situated between Peru and Brazil; they began thenceforth to recover traces of the captors; and it was in the midst of these inextricable woods that Martin Paz recovered all his Indian sagacity.

Courage returned to the Spaniard, strength returned to Liberta, when a half-extinct fire and prints of footsteps proved the proximity of their enemies. Martin Paz noted all and studied all, the breaking of the little branches, the nature of the vestiges.

Don Vegal feared lest his unfortunate daughter should have been dragged on foot through the stones and thorns; but the Indian showed him some pebbles strongly imbedded in the earth, which indicated the pressure of an animal's foot; above, branches had been pushed aside in the same direction, which could have been reached only by a person on horseback. The poor father comforted himself and recovered life and hope, and then Martin Paz was so confident, so skillful, so strong, that there were for him neither impassable obstacles nor insurmountable perils.

Nevertheless immense forests contracted the horizon around them, and trees multiplied incessantly before their fatigued eyes.

One evening, while the darkness was gathering beneath the opaque foliage, Martin Paz, Liberta and Don Vegal were compelled by fatigue to stop. They had reached the banks of a river; it was the river Madeira, which the Indian recognized perfectly; immense mangrove trees bent above the sleeping wave and were united to the trees on the opposite shore by capricious *lianes* (vines), on which were balancing the *titipaying* and the *concoulies*.

Had the captors ascended the banks? had they descended the course of the river? had they crossed it in a direct line? Such were the questions with which Martin Paz puzzled himself. He stepped a little aside from his companions, following with infinite difficulty some fugitive tracks; these brought him to a clearing a little less gloomy. Some footsteps indicated that a company of men had, perhaps, crossed the river at this spot, which was the opinion of the Indian, although he found around him no proof of the construction of a canoe; he knew that the Sambo might have cut down some tree in the middle of the forest, and having spoiled it of its bark, made of it a boat, which could have been carried on the arms of men to the shores of the Madeira. Nevertheless, he was still hesitating, when he saw a sort of black mass move near a thicket; he quickly prepared his lasso and made ready for an attack; he advanced a few paces, and perceived an animal lying on the ground, a prey to the final convulsions—it was a mule. The poor, expiring beast had been struck at a distance from the spot whither it had been dragged, leaving long traces of blood on its passage. Martin Paz no longer doubted that the Indians, unable to induce it to cross the river, had killed it with the stroke of a poignard, as a deep wound indicated. From this moment he felt certain of the direction of his enemies; and returned to his companions, who were already uneasy at his long absence.

"To-morrow, perhaps, we shall see the young girl!" said he to them.

"My daughter! Oh! my son! let us set out this instant," said the Spaniard; "I am no longer fatigued, and strength returns with hope—let us go!"

"But we must cross this river, and we cannot lose time in constructing a canoe."

"We will swim across."

"Courage, then, my father! Liberta and myself will sustain you."

All three laid aside their garments, which Martin Paz carried in a bundle upon his head; and all three glided silently into the water, for fear of awakening some of these dangerous *caïmans* so numerous in the rivers of Brazil and Peru.

They arrived safely at the opposite shore: the first care of Martin Paz was to recover traces of the Indians; but in vain did he scrutinize the smallest leaves, the smallest pebbles—he could discover nothing; as the rapid current had carried them down in crossing, he ascended the bank of the river to the spot opposite that where he had found the mule, but nothing indicated the direction taken by the captors. It must have been that these, that their tracks might be entirely lost, had descended the river for several miles, in order to land far from the spot of their embarkation.

Martin Paz, that his companions might not be discouraged, did not communicate to them his fears; he said not even a word to Don Vegal respecting the mule, for fear of saddening him still more with the thought that his daughter must now be dragged through these difficult passes.

When he returned to the Spaniard, he found him asleep—fatigue had prevailed over grief and resolution; Martin Paz was careful not to awaken him; a little sleep might do him much good; but, while he himself watched, resting the head of Don Vegal on his knees and piercing with his quick glances the surrounding shadows, he sent Liberta to seek below on the river some trace which might guide them at the first rays of the sun.

The Indian departed in the direction indicated, gliding like a serpent between the high brush with which the shores were bristling, and the sound of his footsteps was soon lost in the distance.

Thenceforth Martin Paz remained alone amid these gloomy solitudes: the Spaniard was sleeping peacefully; the names of his daughter and the Indian sometimes mingled in his dreams, and alone disturbed the silence of these obscure forests.

The young Indian was not mistaken; the Sambo had descended the Madeira three miles, then had landed with the young girl and his numerous companions, among whom might be numbered Manangani, still covered with hideous wounds.

The company of Sambo had increased during the journey. The Indians of the plains and the mountains had awaited with impatience the triumph of the revolt; on learning the failure of their brethren, they fell prey to a gloomy despair; hearing that they had been betrayed by Martin Paz, they uttered yells of rage; when they saw that they had a victim to be sacrificed to their anger, they burst forth in cries of joy and followed the company of the old Indian.

They marched thus to the approaching sacrifice, devouring the young girl with sanguinary glances—it was the betrothed, the beloved of Martin Paz whom they were about to put to death; abuse was heaped upon her, and more than once the Sambo, who wished his revenge to be public, with difficulty wrested Sarah from their fury.

The young girl, pale, languishing, was without thought and almost without life amid this frightful horde; she had no longer the sentiment of motion, of will, of existence—she advanced, because bloody hands urged her onward; they might have abandoned her in the midst of these great solitudes—she could not have taken a step to have escaped death. Sometimes the remembrance of her father and of the young Indian passed before her eyes, but like a gleam of lightning bewildering her; then she fell again an inert mass on the neck of the poor mule, whose wounded feet could no longer sustain her. When beyond the river she was compelled to follow her captors on foot, two Indians taking her by the arm dragged her rapidly along, and a trace of blood marked on the sand and dead leaves her painful passage.

But the Sambo was no longer afraid of pursuit; he cared little that this blood betrayed the direction he had taken—he was approaching the termination of his journey, and soon the cataracts which abound in the currents of the great river sent up their deafening clamor.

The numerous company of Indians arrived at a sort of village, composed of a hundred huts, made of reeds interlaced and clay; at their approach, a multitude of women and children darted toward them with loud cries of joy—more than one found there his anxious family—more than one wife missed the father of her children!

These women soon learned the defeat of their party; their sadness was transformed into rage on learning the defection of Martin Paz, and on seeing his betrothed devoted to death.

Sarah remained immovable before these enemies and looked at them with a dim eye; all these hideous faces were making grimaces around her, and the most terrific threats were uttered in her ears—the poor child might have thought herself delivered over to the torturers of the infernal regions.

"Where is my husband?" said one; "it is thou who hast caused him to be killed!"

"And my brother, who will never again return to the cabin—what hast thou done with him? Death! death! Let each of us have a piece of her flesh! let each of us have a pain to make her suffer! Death! death!"

And these women, with dishevelled hair, brandishing knives, waving flaming brands, bearing enormous stones, approached the young girl, surrounded her, pressed her, crushed her.

It was a risky action to pass these mountains.

"Back!" cried the Sambo, "back! and let all await the decision of their chiefs! This girl must disarm the anger of the Great Spirit, which has rested upon our arms; and she shall not serve for private revenge alone!"

The women obeyed the words of the old Indian, casting frightful glances on the young girl; the latter, covered with blood, remained extended on the pebbly shore.

Above this village, plunges, from a height of more than a hundred feet, a foaming cataract, which breaks against sharp rocks; the Madeira, contracted into a deep bed, precipitates this dense mass of water with frightful rapidity; a cloud of mist is eternally suspended above this torrent, whose fall sends its formidable and thundering roar afar.

It was in the midst of this foaming tempest that the unfortunate young girl was destined to die; at the first rays of the sun, exposed in a bark canoe above the cataract, she was to be precipitated with the mass of waters on the rude rocks against which the Madeira broke.

So the council of chiefs had decided; and they had delayed until the morrow the punishment of their victim, to give her a night of anguish, of torment, and of terror.

When the sentence was made known, cries of joy welcomed it, and a furious delirium seized the Indians.

It was a night of orgies—a night of blood and of horror; brandy increased the excitement of these wild natives; dances, accompanied with perpetual yells, surrounded the young girl, and wound their fantastic chains about the stake to which she was fastened. Sometimes the circle narrowed, and enlaced her in its furious whirls: the Indians ran through the uncultivated fields, brandishing blazing pine-branches, and surrounding the victim with light.

And it was thus until sunrise, and worse yet when its first rays illuminated the scene. The young girl was detached from the stake, and a hundred arms were stretched out to drag her to execution, when the name of Martin Paz involuntarily escaped her lips, and cries of hatred and of vengeance responded.

It was necessary to climb by steep paths the immense pile of rocks which led to the upper level of the river, and the victim arrived there all bloody; a canoe of bark awaited her a hundred paces above the fall; she was deposited in it, and fastened by bonds which entered her flesh.

"Vengeance and death!" exclaimed the whole tribe, with one voice.

The canoe was hurried on with increasing rapidity and began to whirl.

Suddenly a man appeared on the opposite shore— It is Martin Paz! Beside him, are Don Vegal and Liberta.

"My daughter! my daughter!" exclaims the father, kneeling on the shore.

"My father!" replied Sarah, raising herself up with superhuman strength.

The scene was indescribable. The canoe was rapidly hastening to the cataract, in whose foam it was already enveloped.

Martin Paz, standing on a rock, balanced his lasso which whistled around his head. At the instant the boat was about to be precipitated, the long leathern thong unfolded from above the head of the Indian, and surrounded the canoe with its noose.

"My daughter! my daughter!" exclaimed Don Vegal.

"My betrothed! my beloved!" cried Martin Paz.

"Death!" yelled the savage multitude.

Meanwhile Martin Paz redoubles his efforts; the canoe remains suspended over the abyss; the current cannot prevail over the strength of the young Indian; the canoe is drawn to him; the enemies are far on the opposite shore; the young girl is saved.

Suddenly an arrow whistles through the air, and pierces the heart of Martin Paz. He falls forward in the bark of the victim; and, re-descending the current of the river in her arms, is engulfed with Sarah in the vortex of the cataract.

A yell of triumph is heard above the sound of the torrent.

Liberta bore off the Spaniard amid a cloud of arrows, and disappeared with him.

Don Vegal regained Lima, where he died with grief and exhaustion.

The Sambo, who remained among his sanguinary tribes, was never heard of more.

The Jew Samuel kept the hundred thousand piasters he had received, and continued his usuries at the expense of the Limanian nobles.

Martin Paz and Sarah were, in their brief and final re-union, betrothed for eternity.

THE END

✠

Illustrations

ONE OF THE CHALLENGES in the Palik series is selecting illustrations. Most are derived from the first French publication of Verne stories in the 19th century and the beginning of the 20th century. They are selected either from the stories with which they appeared, or from others, choosing images to match the new context, with the source work noted in the captions. Only those depicting actual historical locales, persons or events are from other sources, such as the maps from *Garibaldi's Defense of the Roman Republic*, by George Macaulay Trevelyan, first published in 1907.

The publication here of *Martin Paz* includes, for the first time in an English-language edition, the eleven illustrations from the *Musée des familles* publication, by E. Forest, E. Berton and C. Brux, together with the nine illustrations by Jules-Descartes Férat and three by an anonymous hand, for the Hetzel edition.

We are particularly indebted to Bernhard Krauth, chairman of the German Jules-Verne-Club since 2005, for providing the illustrations from Verne stories. A deep sea licensed master working today as a docking pilot in Bremerhaven, Germany, Bernhard has published several Verne-related articles in France, the Netherlands and Germany. Intensely interested in the illustrations of the original French editions of Verne's work, he has been deeply involved in a project to digitize the illustrations, more than 5,000 in all. The project is for common, non-commercial use, and most of the illustrations in the Palik series were made possible through his generosity.

Additional thanks are due to J.A. Marquis for assistance in providing scans of covers of the original Hetzel volumes of Verne stories. Scans from various editions have been provided by Frits Roest of Het Jules Verne Genootschap (the Dutch Verne Society).

✠

Acknowledgements

THE PALIK SERIES, while spearheaded by the North American Jules Verne Society, represents a cooperative effort among Vernians worldwide, pooling the resources and knowledge of the various organizations in different countries. Ariel Perez and Jan Rychlík provided assistance with the translations based on their experience and knowledge of the Spanish and Czech editions of these stories. The Society is grateful for research assistance to Frédéric Jaccaud, curator of Jean-Michel Margot's Verne Collection at the Maison d'Ailleurs (House of Elsewhere) in Yverdon-les-Bains, Switzerland. Volker Dehs has shared his knowledge of the author and Verne texts as an ongoing basis for this series.

The City of Nantes (France), whose Municipal Library has placed all Jules Verne manuscripts online, helped make this publication possible, and the Society would like to thank the City of Nantes and its Bibliothèque municipale (Agnès Marcetteau, director) for their ongoing assistance.

The Society also appreciates the efforts of members who have contributed to this volume, including Brian Kutzera, Malcolm Henderson, George Slusser and Mark Eckell. The late Norman Wolcott donated his scan of the 1852 translation of *Martin Paz—The Pearl of Lima* for the Society's use in the Palik series. Other friends of the Society have helped, including Larry Brooks, leader of the yahoo group, Disney's 20,000 Leagues Under the Sea; David March, of The Life and Work of Rafael Sabatini website, and Thomas Mann, chair of the Washington

D.C. chapter of the League of Extraordinary Gentleman. Further assistance has been provided by Jean Frodsham, Elvira Berkowitsch, and Pachara Yongvongpaibul.

✝

Contributors

EDWARD BAXTER is a graduate of Mount Allison University and the University of Toronto, and has also studied at the University of Lausanne. He taught French for nearly thirty years at Ontario secondary schools. From 1977 until retiring in 1986, Baxter was Head of Modern Languages at Don Mills Collegiate Institute in North York, where he was appointed for a one-year term in 1980 as the city's first Poet Laureate. Baxter has translated several hundred articles for the *Dictionary of Canadian Biography*, along with eight books. These include two distinguished new versions of Verne's *Family Without a Name* (1982) and *The Fur Country* (1987), both sponsored under the auspices of the Canada Council, published by the New Canada Press. After translating "The Humbug" for *The Jules Verne Encyclopedia* (Scarecrow Press, 1996), Baxter contributed a series of new Verne translations for several publishers: *The Invasion of the Sea* (Wesleyan, 2001), *The Golden Volcano* (Nebraska, 2008), and the 1882 play *Journey Through the Impossible* (2003), copublished by Prometheus and the North American Jules Verne Society. For the Palik Series, Baxter has translated not only the present volume, but also Verne's novel, *The Count of Chanteleine: A Tale of the French Revolution*, and "The Marriage of Mr. Anselme des Tilleuls" for the volume, *The Marriage of a Marquis*.

DANIEL COMPÈRE has been professor of literature at the University of Sorbonne Nouvelle-Paris III since 1995. A specialist in Verne, he has published numerous articles on the author and such books as *Jules Verne écrivain* (Geneva: Droz, 1991) and *Les Voyages extraordinaires* *de Jules Verne* (Paris: Pocket, 2005). Compère is also interested in many other writers of the 19th and 20th centuries, such as Victor Hugo, Émile Zola, Albert Robida, Raymond Queneau, Jacques Prévert, and Georges Perec. Compère's publications devoted to popular literature include an encyclopedic work, *Les Maîtres du fantastique en littérature* (Paris: Bordas, 1993) and two books on Alexandre Dumas. He edits the journal *Le Rocambole,* devoted to various aspects of the popular novel, and in 2007 edited *Dictionnaire du roman populaire francophone* (Paris: Nouveau Monde Edition), containing 500 articles on the popular novel of the early 19th century to today.

BRIAN TAVES (Ph.D., University of Southern California) has been an archivist in the Motion Picture, Broadcasting, and Recorded Sound Division of the Library of Congress since 1990. He is the author of over 100 articles and 25 chapters in anthologies. Taves has also written books on P.G. Wodehouse and Hollywood; director Robert Florey; the genre of historical adventure movies; and fantasy-adventure writer Talbot Mundy, in addition to editing an original anthology of Mundy's best stories. In 2002-2003, Taves was chosen as Kluge Staff Fellow at the Library to write the first book on silent film pioneer Thomas Ince, published in 2011. Taves's writing on Verne has been translated into French, German, and Spanish, and he is currently writing a book on the 300 film and television adaptations of Verne worldwide. Taves is coauthor of *The Jules Verne Encyclopedia* (Scarecrow, 1996), and editor of the first English-language publication of Verne's *Adventures of the Rat Family* (Oxford, 1993).

✛

The Palik Series

THE LAST TWO DECADES have brought astonishing progress in the study of Jules Verne, with new translations of Verne stories, including the discovery of many texts. Still, there remain a number of Verne stories that have been overlooked, and it is this gap that the North American Jules Verne Society seeks to fill in the Palik series.

The North American Jules Verne Society (NAJVS) was formed in 1993, and a decade later, underwrote *Journey Through the Impossible*, the first complete edition in any language of Verne's 1882 science fiction theatrical spectacle, *Voyage à travers l'impossible*. With this experience, and thanks to the generosity of the Society's late member, Edward Palik, a series was commenced to bring to the Anglophone public a series of hitherto unknown Verne tales.

Ed Palik had a special enthusiasm for bringing neglected Verne stories to English-speaking readers, and this will be reflected in the series that bears his name. In this way the Society hopes to fulfill the goal that Ed's consideration has made possible, along with the assistance of a variety of Verne translators and scholars from around the world. The volumes in the Palik series will reveal the amazing range of Verne's storytelling, in genres that may surprise those who only know his most famous stories. We hope to allow a better appreciation of the famous writer who has, for more than a century and a half, been the widest-read author of fiction in the world.

PREVIOUS VOLUMES IN THE PALIK SERIES:

The Marriage of a Marquis

Jules Verne is the acclaimed author of such pioneering science fiction as *20,000 Leagues Under the Sea* and *Journey to the Center of the Earth*. Yet he also wrote much more, and foreshadowing such classics as *Around the World in 80 Days*, this inaugural volume focuses on two of Verne's earliest humorous stories, *The Marriage of Mr. Anselme des Tilleuls* and *Jédédias Jamet, or The Tale of an Inheritance*. Translation is provided by Edward Baxter and Kieran O'Driscoll, two of the leading Verne experts; critical commentary by Jean-Michel Margot, Walter James Miller, and Brian Taves examines both stories, and scholars explore why some of the author's stories were overlooked for so many years.

Shipwrecked Family: Marooned with Uncle Robinson

Castaway by pirates on a deserted island… without tools or supplies to survive… a mother and her children have only a kindly old sailor to help. But what explains the strange flora and fauna they find?

The second volume in the Palik series was rejected by Verne's publisher, so rather than finish it, he began to rewrite it with new characters—and that became the classic, *The Mysterious Island*, where Captain Nemo made his last appearance. Here, then, is Verne's first draft of that novel, one which is very different from the book that it became.

Translation is provided by Sidney Kravitz, also translator of the definitive modern edition of *The Mysterious Island* (Wesleyan University Press, 2002). The introduction by Brian Taves discusses the influence of the Robinsonade on Verne's oeuvre, while an appendix comprises Verne's own prefaces to two of his novels in the genre, describing the influence of the form on his writing.

Mr. Chimp and Other Plays

Long before Verne stories had formed the basis for such movies as *Around the World in 80 Days*, many of his plays were theatrical blockbusters on the 19th century stage, including several from his novels. Even as he became a novelist, the stage remained crucial to Verne. In this volume, expert scholarly research by Jean-Michel Margot introduces four of Verne's plays written in his youth, translated by Frank Morlock. Included are *The Knights of the Daffodil, Mr. Chimpanzee, An Adoptive Son*, and *Eleven Days of Siege*, and Verne's collaborators were Michel Carré, Charles Wallut and Victorien Sardou. The works range in content from romantic comedies to a scientist's discovery that there may not be such a difference between human and ape after all!

The Count of Chanteleine: A Tale of the French Revolution
This adventure is for everyone who has thrilled to *The Scarlet Pimpernel*, *A Tale of Two Cities*, or *Scaramouche*. A nobleman, the Count of Chanteleine, leads a rebellion against the revolutionary French government. While he fights for the monarchy and the church, his home is destroyed and his wife murdered by the mob. Now he must save his daughter from the guillotine. This exciting swashbuckler is also a meticulous historical re-creation of a particularly bloody episode in the Reign of Terror.

Commentary by an international team of experts including Garmt de Vries-Uiterweerd, Volker Dehs and Brian Taves explores the historical background, composition, and generic context of *The Count of Chanteleine*, translated by Edward Baxter.

Vice, Redemption and the Distant Colony
Literary fraud or filial devotion? This is the question at the heart of a firestorm that erupted when manuscripts and letters were discovered proving that Jules Verne's son, Michel, significantly revised over a dozen of the stories published under his father's name, and even originated some himself. It was a collaboration that had begun while both were still alive, and continued as Michel saw to the posthumous publication of many of his father's books.

In this volume will be found two different versions of a story, as written by Jules (*Pierre-Jean*), and expanded by his son (into *The Somber Fate of Jean Morénas*)—a tale Michel even made as a movie in 1916! Also in these pages is the first English translation of a novel Jules began, *Fact-Finding Mission*, but which his son finished, and hitherto has been only available in the completed version by Michel Verne.

The English rendering and notes are by a leading authority on Verne translations, Kieran O'Driscoll.

Around the World in 80 Days—The 1874 Play
Jules Verne's most famous novel was originally conceived as a play—and had its greatest 19ᵗʰ century success as a stage hit the author

himself adapted. Running for thousands of performances in many different countries, including the United States, here is the original playscript, translated directly from the French by the producers of the original Broadway presentation, and not published since 1874. Like filmmakers after him, Verne understood the need to make changes for the stage, and in collaboration with Adolphe d'Ennery created a distinct variation, a play with many different characters and episodes than are in the novel. Included in this volume are an introduction about how the play was created and staged, together with the first translation of Verne's essay, "The Meridians and the Calendar," by Jean-Louis Trudel, explaining how Phileas Fogg accomplished his feat. Background on the production of the play, especially its staging in the United States, is provided by Philippe Burgaud, Jean-Michel Margot, and Brian Taves, along with an appendix on films of the play.

Additional volumes are underway.

In 2003, the North American Jules Verne Society also co-published (with Prometheus) the Verne play, *Journey Through the Impossible*. A tale of fantasy and science fiction, *Journey Through the Impossible* ran for 97 performances in Paris in 1882 and 1883. In three acts, the characters go first to the center of the Earth, then under the sea, and finally into outer space to the planet Altor. Characters from *Journey to the Center of the Earth, From the Earth to the Moon, Twenty Thousand Leagues under the Sea*, and *A Fancy of Doctor Ox* appear again in *Journey through the Impossible*. The players include Captain Nemo, the lunar travelers Barbicane and Michel Ardan, Doctor Ox, and Professor Lidenbrock, after his trip to the center of the earth. Translation of *Journey Through the Impossible* is by Edward Baxter, with introduction and notes by Jean-Michel Margot, along with reviews from the play's first presentation. Roger Leyonmark provides new illustrations in the style of the 19th century woodcuts that first illustrated French editions of Verne works, and the original engravings from the play are also featured. This is the first complete edition and English translation of a surprising work, by the popular French novelist whose works continue to delight readers—and audiences—to this day.

✛

For additional details, and links to order the books, see the North American Jules Verne Society's website: www.najvs.org.

9 781593 933951